MURDER IN THE GILDED CAGE

MURDER IN THE GILDED CAGE

SAMUEL SPEWACK

Originally published in 1929.

Published by Wildside Press.

Visit us online at wildsidepress.com.

INTRODUCTION
KARL WURF

When Samuel Spewack penned *Murder in the Gilded Cage* in the late 1920s, he created a quintessential Golden Age mystery that captures both the glamour and the moral decay of America's upper class in the aftermath of the First World War. This novel stands as a fascinating artifact of its era—a time when divorce scandals commanded front-page headlines, when the nouveau riche built palatial winter homes in Havana, and when the reading public's appetite for sensational crime seemed insatiable.

Samuel Spewack (1899–1971) would become best known for his theatrical collaborations with his wife, Bella, particularly their musical adaptation of Shakespeare's *The Taming of the Shrew* into the smash hit *Kiss Me, Kate*. But before his Broadway triumphs, Spewack worked as a journalist, and that background permeates every page of this novel. The unnamed narrator—a press agent who finds himself reluctantly employed by the scandal-plagued Mrs. Breese—serves as Spewack's vehicle for a knowing, cynical examination of how the media both creates and feeds upon public sensation. The book's journalistic sensibility extends beyond its narrator. Spewack writes with the clipped, efficient prose of a newspaperman, and his plot unfolds with the pacing of a serialized story designed to keep readers turning pages. Yet beneath the surface entertainment lies a sharp social commentary on class, wealth, and the compromises people make in pursuit of both.

Murder in the Gilded Cage belongs firmly to the Golden Age of Detective Fiction, that period roughly spanning from 1920 to 1939 when the genre codified many of its most enduring conventions. Like Agatha Christie, Dorothy L. Sayers, and their contemporaries, Spewack presents readers with a closed circle of suspects—in this case, the members of Mrs. Breese's household aboard her yacht and in her Havana mansion. The solution demands careful attention to detail, alibis, and the psychological motivations of each character. However, Spewack adds his own distinctive elements to the formula. Boris Sergeivitch Perutkin, the displaced Russian detective who becomes instrumental to solving the case, brings an exotic, melancholic quality to the investigation. A former agent of the Czarist secret police, Perutkin represents the old European order swept away by revolution, now reduced to pursuing a six-year-old murder case as a matter of personal honor rather than official duty. His presence adds a layer of historical gravitas to what might otherwise be a straightforward society mystery.

The novel's title provides its central metaphor. Mrs. Breese's magnificent Havana palace, dubbed "the Gilded Cage" by malicious wits, represents the trap of wealth and social position. The various characters find themselves imprisoned by their own desires, their need for money, their hunger for status, or their fear of scandal. Guy Thomas, the young actor kept by Mrs. Breese, is the most obvious bird in this cage, but Spewack suggests that everyone in the household is trapped in their own way. The book also offers a fascinating portrait of the 1920s obsession with publicity and celebrity. Mrs. Breese's need to remain in the public eye even after her divorce trial has ended drives much of the plot. In an era before reality television and social media, the newspapers served as the primary vehicle for fame, and Spewack's narrator—himself a professional manipulator of public opinion—provides an insider's view of how scandal is manufactured and maintained.

Gender and power dynamics receive sharp examination throughout the narrative. Mrs. Breese, described as a woman with a "Napoleonic complex," wields her wealth and forceful personality to control those around her. Yet the book also exposes the limitations of her power in a male-dominated society. Her daughter, the Countess, represents a younger generation caught between old-world aristocracy and new-world pragmatism, while the various men in the story—from the weak-willed Thomas to the forceful Gordon Rice—each respond differently to female wealth and authority.

Modern readers approaching *Murder in the Gilded Cage* should be prepared for the conventions and attitudes of its era. The prose style, while economical, reflects the period's more formal diction. Character psychology is drawn in broader strokes than contemporary readers might expect. The book's treatment of servants, particularly the "Japanese" and "half-caste" staff members, reveals the casual racism typical of the period, though Spewack's attitude toward his upper-class characters is consistently more critical than admiring. Yet the book remains remarkably fresh in many ways. Its cynicism about the wealthy, its understanding of how media shapes public perception, and its portrait of people trapped by their own choices all resonate with contemporary concerns. The mystery plot, while constructed along classical lines, offers sufficient twists and surprises to engage modern mystery fans. Spewack plays fair with his readers, providing all the necessary clues while still managing to misdirect attention effectively.

The international setting adds considerably to the book's appeal. The transition from New York to the yacht to Havana allows Spewack to paint varied backdrops for his drama. His portrait of Havana in the late 1920s—before the Revolution, during America's quasi-colonial relationship with Cuba—offers historical interest beyond the mystery plot. The city appears as a playground for wealthy Americans, a place where normal social rules might be suspended, making it the perfect setting for both romance and murder.

Murder in the Gilded Cage deserves recognition as more than a mere period curiosity. While it may lack the polish and innovation of works by the era's most celebrated mystery writers, it offers compensating virtues: sharp social observation, brisk pacing, and a genuine understanding of how wealth and publicity corrupt human relationships. Spewack's background in journalism gives the book an authenticity that purely literary writers of detective fiction sometimes lacked. For readers interested in the Golden Age of detective fiction, this novel provides an excellent example of how the genre could be used for social commentary. For those fascinated by the 1920s, it offers a vivid snapshot of upper-class American life in the years before the Great Depression would sweep away much of the world it depicts. And for anyone who simply enjoys a well-constructed mystery with memorable characters and an exotic setting, *Murder in the Gilded Cage* delivers thoroughly satisfying entertainment.

CHAPTER I
MRS. BREESE IS DIVORCED

I HAVE JUST returned to New York and examined in the morgue of the New York Times all the stories written and cabled of the Murder in the Gilded Cage. It is now six months since the weird death of Mrs. Breese, and I have decided that it is to the public interest that I present an unbiased factual account of what actually occurred in her winter home. For it is high time that someone set at rest the malicious rumors that still buzz wherever her set gathers. It is certainly due three of the principal actors in the tragedy that the truth be known. Whatever their personal failings may be, they have done nothing to deserve the stigma attached to their names. I do not see eye to eye with Ben Smith on this matter, who is responsible for the hitherto impenetrable secrecy. Boris Sergeivitch Perutkin, that most fantastic of investigators, is now concerned with another and even more devious problem, and does not care.

Perhaps it would be best to set forth first my connection with the case. You may remember that Mrs. Breese, before her storied death, was the center of a divorce case that startled the country. There is no need here to rake the dead leaves of sensation. It was one of those cases that linger on to the profit of lawyers over a period of years and supply the tabloids with juicy drippings. When it was all over, Mrs. Breese won. Her husband, in disgusted settlement, gave her the Havana home, the yacht, *Mary Rose*, named for their daughter, a coöperative Park Avenue apartment, and a competence that came to some fifty thousand dollars a year. Mrs. Breese's lawyers fared even better. I might mention that Mrs. Breese was independently wealthy in addition, although her legal representatives went to some pains to conceal the fact. In any case, the scandal drove her out of the enigmatic pages of the Social Register and made her for the time being one of the best known women in America.

You will remember, too, that the name of Guy Thomas was coupled with hers all during the tortuous trials and appeals. Mr. Breese named him as co-respondent, although all efforts to prove the accusation were unsuccessful. Mutual friends of the Breeses divided on this issue. Gordon Rice, for example, in characteristic hearty fashion, refused to believe a word of it and severed a relationship of thirty years' standing with the husband. Mr. Rice said Guy Thomas was a pleasant young man and an excellent dancer, which Mr. Breese was not, and he'd be hanged if he'd stand by and see an innocent woman spattered with scandal because of an entirely harmless friendship with a personable young actor.

When I set forth as a reporter for the News Association to cover the trial, I flattered myself on a professional lack of opinion in the matter. I did not know then that I would be thrown bodily into the maze of Mrs. Breese's post-divorce life; and her perplexing death. Why I ever entered the service of Mrs. Breese I do not know. Ben Smith thinks it was sheer laziness and the inability to refuse. Perhaps it was because the woman fascinated me as a creature of incredibility. Yet she was real enough. But let me tell the story from the beginning. You shall judge for yourself.

With the aid of a newspaper clipping, I establish April 17, 1928 as the date of my first meeting with Mrs. Breese. I had come up from Richmond several weeks before, and finally found a berth with a local news agency. The case was totally unfamiliar to me when I set out to interview Mrs. Breese a day before her trial was scheduled to begin.

It was a glorious afternoon, a rare April day, and even the ornate lobby of the Park Avenue apartment house permitted an occasional beam of sun to enter. After preliminary negotiations with the doorman, the telephone operator, and the elevator guards, I was permitted to ascend to the fourteenth story, where a butler conducted me from the reception-hall to the high-ceilinged drawing-room. There were five enormous windows, and every shade was drawn, so that you had the impression of sitting in one of those softly-carpeted motion picture palaces. Later I was to discover that Mrs. Breese flowered only in dim rooms, with shades and curtains drawn, and her idea of human habitation was in harmony with that of the designers of the motion picture temples. She carried this atmosphere wherever she went, as people will.

She made a dramatic entrance into the room after keeping me waiting fully fifteen minutes, and I could hear her voice behind the grilled door, a peculiarly harsh voice that trilled, curiously enough, and chattered.

"SO sorry to keep you waiting," the voice said before I saw her, and then a tall and full-bosomed figure in jade green swept before me. Even in the faint light I could see she was a blonde, with somewhat faded blue eyes. It took no discerning observer to note that the masseur and the hairdresser had preceded me, and that the ladies' maid had done her daily stint. The air filled not unpleasantly with a rare perfume, and then, with a gracious gesture to me, the lady seated herself, poised for the ordeal.

But if I expected a reticent, an embarrassment quite natural under the circumstances, I was quickly disillusioned. Despite newspaper training, I was bred in the school that regards one's private life as unfit for public discussion. I expected to sympathize with her on the unfortunate circumstances that compelled me to intrude. But she made that quite unnecessary, in the harsh trilling voice that I shall never forget.

"My husband," she said, "has a Napoleonic complex. He thinks he can dominate me." She paused. "He can't." I readily believed that, although I had never met Mr. Breese. I might explain that Mrs. Breese had but recently discovered psychoanalysts, and the jargon of their trade was always on the tip of her tongue.

She then plunged into a detailed résumé of her grievances, which were many. She spoke with a cold vindictiveness that was repellent, and yet with a certain relish. I was to discover soon that Mrs. Breese, instead of shrinking from the publicity of the scandal, gloried in it. Who can forget the first day of her trial when the decrepit State Court Building was mobbed by the curious? For that event she had seated herself beside her chauffeur in the baby-blue limousine. She wore a bright plaid skirt, a Russian blouse, and about her head she had bound a bright bandanna handkerchief. "It is the gypsy in me," she confided later. But if you were to dismiss her as a silly woman, you must ignore the occasional gleam of intelligence that shone from the fog of her chatter. And the occasionally generous impulses that made you think of her as a fine and noble-minded woman who had somehow let her life literally fall to pieces.

Mrs. Breese on the witness stand was meat and drink for the newspapers. She thought in headlines, and just about the time you had decided she was exhausted as a subject, she dragged out something else to feed the flames. Poor Mr. Breese hid from the reporters and smashed photographers' cameras, and although he had been guilty of only a meaningless affair with a Follies beauty of uncertain reputation, lost the case with a resounding thud. And got himself thrown out of clubs, and snubbed by righteous individuals who knew the value of discretion.

Guy Thomas took the stand and absolved Mrs. Breese and himself from all wrong-doing. He was thirty-two then, dark, with that sleek look of a man who gives a good deal of attention to his clothes and his barber. He was singularly handsome, and had once been a model for commercial photographers. That was when he could not find work as an actor. Which was frequently. He was not a good actor. He had met Mrs. Breese at one of those Bohemian parties where social distinctions are wiped out for the evening, and she had taken what I believed at the time to have been a casual interest in him.

He did dance very well. He had a classic regularity of feature, and an excellent chin, and was one of the weakest men I ever met. I cannot explain his actions otherwise. As a type you associate him with Fifth Avenue tailors and Park Avenue restaurants, cheap cigarettes in gold cases, and an extremely limited knowledge of anything transpiring beyond his own immediate world.

Readily enough he admitted that occasionally Mrs. Breese had been good enough to entertain him in certain restaurants in return for his services as cavalier and dancing partner.

"I didn't have the money to take her to such places," he explained with a frank smile and a gleam of white teeth. "We discussed that, and rather than lose the pleasure of taking her out, I agreed she could pay the bills."

There was a titter and some giggles in the courtroom, at which the young man flushed.

"I couldn't take her to the type of restaurants I am forced to dine in occasionally," he added in justification.

On the whole, his testimony did her no harm. If he did not cut a swagger figure, it was the opinion of jury and spectators that entertaining Mrs. Breese was Mr. Breese's task, and in this the husband had obviously been negligent.

The two Breese children, Henry Jr. and the Countess Giering-Trelovitch, testified for their mother. Henry Jr. was twenty and the Countess twenty-five. Henry Jr. swallowed visibly as counsel wrenched from him incidents of bad temper and cruelty of which his father had been guilty. Mrs. Breese cried, rather effectively, while he was on the stand. His father covered his eyes with his hand.

Then the Countess, rather pale, rather bored, and yet curiously lovely, added the necessary confirmation. She seemed a slim edition of her mother, without her mother's enormous energy.

But undoubtedly the star witness was Gordon Rice, wealthy promoter, traveler, and one-time soldier of fortune. Rice was fifty, a few years older than Breese Sr., white-haired, red-faced, and with a downright heartiness of manner that soon won the jury. His was obviously a painful duty, and you felt that the quicker it was over with the better he would like it. He told of the sordid affair of the Follies beauty; how he had warned the elder Breese that it would wreck his marriage. He told of certain episodes that the law demands, and nothing could shake his testimony in the cross-examination.

Then the trial was over, and the verdict was read with great solemnity. After which it was appealed, and appealed again. And then the elder Breese, who refused to take the stand, denied himself to all interviewers, sulked in his hotel suite and instructed the lawyers to settle. They did. And the newspapers, even the tabloids, dropped Mrs. Breese as quickly as they had picked her up.

I had been keeping in touch with her after the trial, for news agencies must continue reporting even the most trivial items long after the newspapers have sent their reporters to greener fields. It was because of this that I was able to observe how unhappy Mrs. Breese had become as interest in her problems waned. Where once the color of a new gown was well-nigh sufficient to warrant a re-make of an edition, her spiciest pronunciamentos now found the waste-basket. Her lawyers advised her to go to Europe and rest. But Mrs. Breese did not want to rest. The dramatic excitement of the trial had only whetted her appetite for the public eye.

It was pathetic to watch her. One morning she telephoned me to come in post-haste. She had been struck with a brilliant idea; she would finance another of the trans-Atlantic flights. It mattered little to her that the movie queen who was to pilot the plane had just about two hours' flying time to her credit. Mrs. Breese did get a paragraph or two on the event before its obvious impracticability was discovered, and she had the satisfaction of viewing her picture and that of the movie actress adorning a lurid half-page in one of the tabloids.

During the following few weeks she made the most startling observations on short skirts, necking, companionate marriage and life beyond the grave—the four staples of sob-sister interviews. But the editors were tired of Mrs. Breese. A certain staleness clung to the name. Even the crowds in the night clubs no longer turned to stare when she descended upon them for a few moments. So one morning she surrendered. I saw that surrender. Several days before, her social secretary had resigned. He—Mrs. Breese always employed male secretaries—said rather brusquely that his position had become ignominious. He was a rather effeminate young man, and had served several distinguished families.

Mrs. Breese, who was not without humor despite her weaknesses, said she really had no further use for a social secretary since society had dropped her. But she did need someone, to quote her words, "who can keep me in touch with public opinion. I'm so interested in what people are really thinking. I mean, the plain people."

It was the most roundabout way of describing a press-agent that I had heard in some time. I said that there were young ladies who would undoubtedly suit her. But she shook her head vigorously. No. She had already made her choice. And that choice, I discovered to my amazement, was none other than myself. I was not flattered. There was something distinctly unpalatable in being Mrs. Breese's amanuensis. I did not mind glorifying a milk company or a portrait painter or even an oil promoter, but press-agent to a divorcée was not yet officially recognized as altogether legitimate. So I declined with thanks.

But Mrs. Breese persisted. She named a salary which was double that I had been receiving. She sketched a tempting itinerary on the yacht *Mary Rose* and, perhaps, knowing my weakness, she outlined a routine of labor that even for me would be child's play. Still I refused.

But a week later circumstances altered my decision. A new city editor who had assigned me to travel as far as the subway penetrates discovered through some mischance that I had used the telephone instead and consumed the allotted time and some excellent Chianti in a neighborhood speakeasy. I received two weeks' salary and a cold dismissal. I went searching for work on the papers without success and soon I could see that the manager of the minor hotel at which I was stopping was beginning to regard me as a problem.

One morning I did not leave my hotel room for breakfast. I had not the courage to face the thin-lipped manager. I sat facing the uninviting court yard, pondering my next move, when the telephone rang suddenly.

"Where in the world have you been?" the harsh, trilling voice of Mrs. Breese demanded, without any preliminary explanation. "I had the most awful time trying to get hold of you. They wouldn't give me your address at your office. Are you in hiding?"

I muttered some lie or other about having been ill. But she obviously was not interested in that.

"Don't you know we're sailing tomorrow? I'm sending Pierre down for your luggage."

I tried to say something, but she continued relentlessly: "Now, it's no use your saying you can't come. You've simply got to! I need you. Now will you come up here at once? There are a million things I've got to talk to you about. And do have your luggage ready. Pierre has just started out."

This woman who took things for granted hung up without waiting for further word from me.

I was in no situation to protest in any case. So I descended at once to the manager and informed him with an off-hand gesture that I had consented to accept a fabulous salary as publicity engineer to a wealthy lady, and consumed on credit a hearty breakfast. I must have been convincing for I left the hotel with five dollars borrowed from the manager and rode up to the Park Avenue ménage in one of those new and immaculate black and white taxis. After weeks of uncertainty the sense of well-being was rather pleasant.

And when I appeared before Mrs. Breese she smiled at me and said: "I knew I could rely on you. I haven't much time, and neither have you. I want you to tell the newspapers that we're sailing tomorrow on the *Mary Rose*.

"I'll give you a list of the guests: Mrs. Henry Breese, Sr. and her two children, Henry Breese, Jr., and the Countess Giering-Trelovitch. Please don't forget the hyphen. Newspapers are so careless. The children have been upset by all this trial and a rest will do them good. Then Mr. Rice—Mr. Gordon Rice—has consented to come along. Mr. Rice, you know, is managing my affairs. You've met him, but you don't really know him. He's a friend—a true friend. I don't know what I should have done without him. You know he was Henry's friend when I first met him. But he didn't let that stand in the way of telling the truth. And now that I've got my affairs to manage he is taking them off my hands. Just think of it! A man whose time is so valuable giving up weeks and weeks just for me! That sort of friendship gives me strength to go on!"

She spoke as if the world had done her a great wrong, and Rice was her only bulwark. "Then I've asked Guy Thomas." She paused for effect and I looked up at her.

"I can see by your face you don't approve. But, my dear boy, I simply must. If anything can prove that ours is nothing but an ordinary friendship, this will. I want you to be particularly careful how you phrase it. Let me see—oh yes, put it this way: 'Mrs. Henry Breese, Sr., announced that Mr. Guy Thomas had been invited to accompany her and her children to Havana. Mrs. Breese said that she refused to take seriously the gossip which had been proven false in court.' Is that all right?"

I indicated that it wasn't. I pointed out that the most dignified thing she could do would be to sail away in her yacht with no one but her two children as guests, and the less said about anyone else the better.

"But I've already invited Guy!" she wailed. "And I couldn't leave him behind now. Anyway, I don't want to. I like Guy. I'm very fond of Guy. Let them talk if they want to."

It seemed to me then that Mrs. Breese wanted them to talk. If any explanation is necessary for her, it lies, I think, in the fact that by temperament if not by ability she belonged to the stage. Whatever public exhibition her social position afforded her had not satisfied her through the years. Her trial had given her the attention she hungered for, and now she would never be content unless she could remain the center of discussion.

So, despite my objections, Mr. Thomas was duly announced as one of the guests and the next morning the newspapers carried non-committal and carefully-worded stories of the fact. Before we sailed, at Mrs. Breese's request, I summoned the photographers. Mrs. Breese posed alone. Then with her son, Henry Jr., then with the Countess von Giering-Trelovitch (Mrs. Breese said gaily: "Don't forget the hyphen!"). Then another pose with both children.

There was one with Gordon Rice, with my amazing employer looking up at him with an expression that was meant to convey faith and friendly affection.

Over-riding my guarded protests, she laughingly put her arm on Guy Thomas' shoulder and posed with that vindicated co-respondent. There followed a picture with the Captain of her yacht, and for comic relief one with a picturesque sailor, displaying huge tattooed arms. I was the only one that escaped.

When the photographers had left, Mrs. Breese went immediately to her cabin. She was tired.

We sailed one hour later.

CHAPTER II
MAN OVERBOARD

I FIND UPON refreshing my memory that the tragedy really had its beginning on the yacht *Mary Rose*, although no one was aware of it at the time. But the diabolical forces that created it were present and at work then, and to give you a proper understanding of its elements, I must proceed chronologically, from the time the *Mary Rose* made its graceful exit out of the New York harbor.

After settling down in my snug cabin, I discovered the need of some masculine conversation. That session with the photographers and Mrs. Breese had provided all the feminine chatter I could stand. My steward proved a forbidding Jap with a perpetual scowl who gave me no encouragement. I discovered later he understood practically no English. Somewhere in her wanderings, Mrs. Breese had collected him, as she told me, for his scowl. So, somewhat disconsolate, I made my way to the music-room, and there I saw stretched out at his ease upon a silken couch the young man who had fought so valiantly for Mrs. Breese's good name.

I have already indicated that industry is not my forte, but Guy Thomas at ease was a picture that made even me squirm. Every line of his body bespoke self-pampering that would be unseemly in a spoiled child. His hands hung listlessly. His eyes were somnolent. He was smoking a cigarette, but even this effort seemed too much for him, for he dropped it weakly in the tray and shifted slightly for additional comfort. Finally he felt me looking at him and rose slowly. There was a challenge in the vacuous eyes now. He had not yet quite ascertained my status in the ménage. And for that matter I was but vaguely acquainted with his.

"Don't let me disturb you," I pleaded. "I was just wondering if I could rustle up a drink."

"Ring the bell," he drawled, indicating a tiny button set near the couch. I obeyed. He slumped back into his old position on the couch, and the Japanese steward with whom I had held preliminary negotiations appeared.

"Cocktails!" Mr. Thomas commanded, and the scowling servitor nodded and disappeared.

Mr. Thomas suppressed a yawn. Somehow the idea occurred to him that it would be discourteous to sit there in slothful silence. So with obvious reluctance he sat up, and lit another cigarette. I consulted my pipe.

"Where are the others?" I asked after a while.

"Oh, here and there," he drawled. "Dora—Mrs. Breese—generally rests before luncheon. The Countess is up on deck, reading. I don't know where Henry happens to be. He and I aren't exactly on speaking terms."

This was the first I had heard of it, and I suppose my expression indicated as much.

"Oh yes," he nodded, as if in answer to my unspoken query. "He's a nice boy, but he just doesn't understand. He doesn't understand my friendship with his mother. Now you're a man of the world—you'd have no trouble understanding. But a boy like that has curious ideas." He flicked a cigarette. "It's damn annoying!" His face clouded. "It spoils things, you know."

I said nothing, and he continued as if he had finally found a confidant: "I wanted everything to be pleasant, damn it. We can have a jolly fine time on this boat. I've been on it before, but naturally you don't feel very comfortable if the son of your hostess is always looking at you as if you don't belong."

The steward appeared with the cocktails, and refreshment further loosened the tongue of the aggrieved young man.

"You and I ought to be pals," he offered graciously. "I mean to say, we're in the same position. What I mean is, we're going along because Mrs. Breese wants us to, damn it! She likes our company and that's all there is to it. But you'll find out before you're on here very long that that young boy is going to make all kinds of remarks. Lounge lizard! He had the nerve to call me that one time. And he'll be calling you that, too."

I pointed out in embarrassed self-defense that I had come along in a professional capacity. But Mr. Thomas merely smiled.

"Of course, of course," he gestured in dismissal of the excuse. "But Mrs. Breese took you along because she liked you. She really doesn't want a thing, I assure you. Finest woman I ever met. She doesn't expect anything. Why, one night in Paris, I remember I was dog-tired and she wanted to dance and I said 'I'm dog-tired,' and what do you think she did? She said 'In that case, we'll stay home.' Hang it all, there's a woman for you."

I cite Mr. Thomas at vacuous length to give you some idea of his mentality and his attitude. There was no question in my mind that the problem of marriage between Mrs. Breese and himself had not come up. Their relationship was still undetermined.

After the cocktails had been consumed, Gordon Rice joined us. He seemed more florid than ever in checked grey and plus fours. He had evidently been up on deck and his face was wind-blown. He greeted the sight of glasses with an expansive chuckle and I pressed the bell for reinforcements.

"Great weather!" Mr. Rice rubbed his cold hands. "I tell you, there's nothing like an ocean trip to set you right. I've been feeling foggy for the last three months, and one hour on deck has sure made a difference." He sat down heavily. He turned to me. "Well, what are you writing up? Got any big news?"

I laughed and said I didn't expect any more big news. Incidentally, I had determined (to salve my conscience) that part of my job would be to suppress such news as Mrs. Breese thought fit for public consumption. If I could do nothing else, I could at least prevent her from making a fool of herself.

"You'll like Havana in the spring," Mr. Rice assured me. "It's past the season and all that, but it's delightful. I was there all through the summer once. 'Ninety-eight. Our little fracas with Spain. Funny, nobody remembers that war. I guess they'll be forgetting the last one before you know it."

"And they should," said the actor. "Hang it all, who wants to remember the war?"

Mr. Rice looked at the young man with some distaste. I had noted before that he did not quite approve of Mrs. Breese's gigolo. I could sense now a healthy active man's dislike of an idler.

Perhaps the actor felt the antagonism, too, for he protested: "I was in the war myself."

Rice raised his eyebrows half skeptically.

"Not exactly in the war. Spent almost a year drilling in camp. And a fine time I had of it! One of those pests of a second-lieutenant, you know. He and I never got along." Thomas smirked. "Not after I took his girl away from him. Then he tried to make life really miserable. Why, he wouldn't even let me wear the uniform my tailor made. Insisted I put on those terrible togs the quartermaster issued."

I tried to steer Mr. Thomas away from his woes, but with scant success.

"I could have killed that wretch!" he muttered with the first sign of conviction I had heard in his voice since his torture on the witness stand. "I would have, too, if it weren't for the armistice."

"You'd never have the go to kill anyone," Rice laughed in his bluff way. "Too much work." His antagonism now was quite frank. But Thomas only smiled feebly, and said: "I don't know about that. I think a man can stand just so much and no more, and then he's just not responsible for himself, damn it."

Rice looked at him as he would at a particularly unpleasant insect. He took no pains to hide his feelings.

"Having been an officer myself," he said, "my sympathy is all for the lieu-tenant. Probably thought he could make a soldier of you if he tried hard enough."

The conversation was getting embarrassing for me. Suddenly I heard Thomas exclaim as if he had been startled. I looked up. In the doorway stood young Henry Breese. I caught only a fleeting glimpse of the boy's face, but there was vindictive hatred in the flash of his eyes. Then he darted out of my sight.

"Now what did he want to do that for?" Thomas whined. Rice continued to look at him. I didn't know what to say. Fortunately at this moment Mrs. Breese sailed into the room, and in relief even Thomas rose to his feet with some alacrity.

"Someone give me a cocktail!" she demanded gaily, and Rice was the first to reach the shaker, and with quiet ceremony fill and give her a glass of what seemed to me a perfect Martini. "Everybody having a good time? I do want everybody to have a good time." She never waited for an answer. "I've ordered luncheon for one. This sea-air should give you all an appetite. I know I feel perfectly marvellous." I doubt if she had even been on deck.

Thomas said he still had some unpacking to do and excused himself. She smiled sweetly at him, and as he left the room her faded blue eyes seemed to follow him appraisingly.

"I think he's perfectly sweet," she murmured, and I could hear Rice grunt in disapproval. Mrs. Breese frowned.

"Gordon, I don't know what you see in Guy that you don't like, but for my sake you might try to understand him. You know you don't understand him or you'd like him."

"Nothing to understand," muttered Rice. There was a moment's silence. Rice seemed to feel uncomfortable. He said finally that he, too, had some unpacking to superintend, clearly a lame excuse, and left us.

Mrs. Breese sighed.

"I don't know what to do. Gordon is a dear, but he just won't understand there are men who can do something else beside worry about business all day long." She took a Russian cigarette from her vanity case and I lit it for her. "It makes it so embarrassing!"

She turned suddenly to me.

"What would you say if I were to tell you that Guy and I were engaged to be married?"

I thought the woman had no further shocks in store for me and I was stunned. She seemed to enjoy my open-mouthed amazement.

"I know I do things in my own strange way. But I've been thinking deeply about this, I assure you. And I've just about made up my mind. I want you to wireless all the newspapers and tell them that just as soon as we reach Havana, Guy Thomas and I will be married. The decree is final. I'm free to marry if I want to. And Guy has always been free."

I breathed deeply. I shared some of Rice's feelings towards the actor.

"But are you sure it's wise?" Then I added hastily, "Of course, I don't mean your marriage. I don't presume to discuss that. But you know an announcement like that would only confirm your husband's charges. It would only confirm the gossip."

"I can't help that!" Mrs. Breese shook her head obstinately. "It's my husband's own fault. I assure you I never looked at Guy as anything but a nice young man until the trial. But now I've discovered I love him, and nothing the world can say or do will part us."

Mrs. Breese was huskily melodramatic, as if the entire universe at that moment were in conspiracy to deprive her of her true love. "Of course, you'll have to word it very discreetly. You can quote me as saying that through common suffering at the trial, we were thrown together. We discovered that our friendship had ripened into something deeper, more significant."

I nodded miserably.

"I want the world to understand that for twenty-six years I have tried to do my duty as a wife to a man I did not love. I married Henry Breese because my family insisted on it. I made my sacrifice." She looked annoyed at me. "But you're not taking a note!"

"I'll remember every word," I assured her. She seemed doubtful.

"It was through no act of mine that I was freed from my dreadful burden.... I do wish you'd take notes.... Very well ... our union was wrecked despite all my efforts to preserve it for the sake of our children. Mr. Breese wanted to make me an outcast. But there is still some justice in this world, and I was exonerated. I was made free. And in my struggles I discovered that Guy Thomas and I were meant for one another. I still have my life to live, now that I have done my duty to my husband and my children. I intend to capture some happiness for myself.... I don't see how you're going to remember all this.... *Very* well.... Of course, ours will be a companionate marriage.... That is distinctly understood.... There shall be no primitive possession.... Ours will be a union of faith and understanding...."

There is no need to continue. You are acquainted with the rest from the stencils of the newspapers. And then Guy Thomas rejoined us.

"Guy!" Mrs. Breese exclaimed significantly. "I have just announced our engagement!"

I would have sworn that the young man so chosen had no inkling of his good fortune. Certainly, I could see he was dumbfounded. His mouth opened and he smirked idiotically. Then he leaned over and kissed her. I found I could not even murmur congratulations. I felt sure, and do to this day, that Mrs. Breese wasn't thinking of marriage or love or anything else at the moment. She was already glorying in the sensation that would be caused in New York. Newsprint can take hold of human beings with the malevolent claws of a narcotic. For she said: "Now I want you to quote Guy, too. What would you like to say, dear?"

"Eh?" said Guy conclusively. But Mrs. Breese characteristically did not even wait for any profundities from him. She said: "I think all you need from Guy is simply that he, too, believes in the terms of our union, that we were thrown together by our common suffering. Please don't forget that. And———"

"I'd like to say," said Guy, suddenly, "that I'm not leaving the stage."

This thunderbolt made little impression upon either Mrs. Breese or myself.

"Of course not, dear," she soothed. "He's not leaving the stage. I would certainly not let anything interfere with my husband's career."

Thomas nodded sagely. Slowly the full significance of the news began to envelop him and I could see him swell like a toy balloon. Probably he had entertained the thought of marrying a very wealthy woman. But he was not one to take the initiative. His berth as companion was too comfortable to risk ambition. Now that his fondest day dream was reality a foolish grin spread over his classical features and stayed there.

"I think he's so handsome!" Mrs. Breese confided to me while Thomas' grin widened.

Whatever else my employer had to say was cut short by the sudden reappearance of Rice. His face was very red, and his eyes blazed angrily. He strode up to Mrs. Breese and muttered: "I'd like to see you alone, if you don't mind."

Mrs. Breese stared coolly at him. "Anything you have to say to me, Gordon, can be said in front of Guy," she said.

"Well then, I'll say it. What's this nonsense about a marriage? I've just been talking to Henry. Are you mad?"

Mrs. Breese drew back proudly.

"I wish you wouldn't take that tone. If you want an answer to your question, I'm not mad."

"You'll have to prove it to me," Rice snapped. "You realize you're fifty-one years old. This—this fellow"—such utter contempt I had rarely heard—-"is young enough to be your son. He's marrying you for your money. That's as plain as day. You go through with this, and you'll be the laughing-stock of everybody. You won't have a friend in the world."

Mr. Thomas flushed, and murmured: "I say, I say!" much in the character of the aristocratic Englishman he had once portrayed on the road.

"I'm not talking to you!" Rice shut him off curtly.

"I will not have Guy insulted!" Mrs. Breese blazed, and then suddenly she melted. "Oh, Gordon, I don't understand you. I thought you were really a friend—a true friend."

"That's what I'm trying to be," said Rice, and his tones grew softer, too. He swallowed uncomfortably. "You know I wish you all the happiness in the world, Dora. I always have. But you don't want to do this thing. After all, there are the children——"

"I've already told the Countess," Mrs. Breese protested. Mrs. Breese always granted the patent of nobility to her daughter, who had divorced an improvident Baltic nobleman. "And I've told Henry. Of course, Henry was a little upset. He's jealous, naturally. But he'll get over it. Henry is a dear boy."

"I've just spoken to him," said Rice, "and I don't agree with you. You know how he felt in college during the trial. He's had to go through a lot. You know how sensitive he is. He's fond of his father, just as fond as he is of you. But he was loyal to you. Now if you want to have the newspapers barking again, as I suppose you do, that's your look-out. I just want to tell you that I'm against it, and I'll do everything in the world to stop you from throwing your life away."

Mrs. Breese did not answer but turned to me. "Will you go right into the radio room and wireless all the newspapers ... and I do wish you had taken notes."

"You send that story and you'll be accountable to me," Rice moved to block my path.

"No use threatening me," I protested. "I'm in Mrs. Breese's employ and I've got to follow orders." She smiled triumphantly at him. "But I don't have to, if I resign. So, Mrs. Breese, if you don't mind, I'll leave the boat in Havana. I quite agree with Mr. Rice. I don't think I can be of any further use to you."

Mrs. Breese was looking daggers at me. I felt a glow of self-righteousness. After all, I was not in the Guy Thomas class of leeches. Then, just as I had started out of the room there came the sound of excited voices, and to cap them, a shrill wailing scream that startled us all. I leaped through the door and to the deck. Rice was close behind me, and even Thomas moved more quickly than ever before.

An excited sailor was hurling a life belt into the water. I saw the Countess clutching the rail, her face contorted with excitement and horror.

"What's happened?" I asked the first sailor I could stop. But I needed no answer.

As my eyes explored the water, I could discern the slim figure of Henry Breese engulfed in a white-capped wave. He was floating. As the life lines were thrown at him, he made no move to catch at them.

Someone shouted. Someone screamed.

But the figure in the water remained still. For a moment I thought it was the figure of a man already dead. Then I realized sickeningly that he was poising himself with steely resolve for his next and final move. I had never before seen such a deliberate, calm attempt at suicide. Slowly the hands rose out of the water. Slowly the torso moved forward, circling, and then in a flash the figure had dived from view.

I heard Mrs. Breese sob back of me, and as I turned helplessly, her face was not pleasant to see. Her daughter swung at her and her eyes were red with fury.

Then before I was quite aware of it, someone brushed me out of the way. Suddenly I realized that the florid and portly Rice was now in the water and swimming with long even strokes to the spot where I had last seen the boy. I saw Rice dive. I saw him reappear without his burden. I saw him dive again. And then quite close to him the figure of the boy rose to the murky blue surface.

But the boy again vanished. Then Rice, too, disappeared, but this time when he emerged one arm held securely a kicking figure. I saw Rice bend over and deliberately punch the boy until his body was still. Then I remember the sailors dragging the two upon the deck. Mrs. Breese fell sobbing upon her son.

CHAPTER III
THE ACTOR ACTS

A DEFINITE CHANGE WAS apparent in the very feel of that yacht after the events of the morning. Henry Breese had been helped to the cabin by Rice and his mother. I waited for them to reappear but when the scowling Japanese announced lunch, there was no sign of them, nor of my other fellow-passengers. I deliberately wandered through the decks, the music-room, even the corridors, hoping that I would meet someone who could shed light on the boy's crazy adventure. I even tried to pump the crew. But each man fell unaccountably silent, and I could see that orders had been given to stem gossip.

At lunch only Guy Thomas appeared, and he was morose and sullen. The steward plied us with the choicest foods, from caviar and hors d'oeuvres and fresh turtle soup to an over-rich dessert, and he ate steadily on, without a word. I realized that this lunch was designed to celebrate his engagement, and I felt very much of a vulture as I glanced at the empty chairs.

Finally, because I could not stand the silence any longer, I said to Thomas: "Perhaps this isn't the pleasantest subject of the moment, but have you any idea of what happened this morning?"

He was just about to light a cigarette, but held his lighter suspended. His eyes set obstinately. "I've got an idea, all right," he muttered. Then he peered at me suspiciously, as if debating whether he could trust me or not. "I've got more than an idea!"

The verdict seemed favorable.

"Rice put him up to that."

"Put him up to what?" I asked puzzled.

"That suicide rot. They framed it between them!"

"Do you mean to say that the boy deliberately jumped in and waited for Rice to drag him out? But why?"

"Why?" He looked at me pityingly. "To scare Dora, that's why! But they can't fool me. They couldn't talk her out of it, so they wanted to scare her out of it."

"What proof have you got?" I demanded.

"Proof? I don't need any proof." And then sullenly, "They may be getting more than they're bargaining for. I'm not going to stand for anything like that, hang it all! They won't get rid of me that way." He peered at me suspiciously. "You can go back and tell them that. You're on their side."

I protested that I was not on any side, but he rose from the table and left me. Puzzled more than ever, I threw away my cigar and then descended to my cabin. After a while I dismissed the events of the morning and pondered upon my own anomalous situation. Having aligned myself against my employer, I must now swim, walk or work my way back to New York. My prospects did not seem bright once we landed in Havana.

There was a knock at the door, and at my invitation Rice entered. He had changed into a blue business suit, and his made-to-order face showed no trace of his exciting morning.

"Thought I'd come in and talk to you," he began, seating himself on the edge of the cot. "Mrs. Breese is busy at the moment and she delegated me to tell you that she wouldn't need your services after we got to Havana."

I nodded.

"I've got some money here, for salary and your expenses back. I'm sorry the way things have happened. I don't suppose it's particularly pleasant for you, but it hasn't been particularly pleasant for us, either. Now there's one thing I wanted to ask you——" He paused deliberately. "Not a word about what's happened this morning. Will you swear to that?"

I looked at Rice and then was seized by an audacious thought. Curiosity has led me into many difficulties.

"I'll do no such thing," I said flatly. "I'm not bound by any confidence. When I leave this boat, I'll be at liberty to say anything I please."

Rice's blue eyes became agate. "Oh—so?" he considered.

"Yes," I said coolly. "I resigned as Mrs. Breese's press-agent before her son threw himself overboard, or at least tried to." I sought to make my voice mocking. "I wonder if he really tried to."

I saw Rice start.

"What in damnation do you mean by that?"

"Well," I hazarded, "I have reason to believe that you and he have—well, shall I call it an understanding?—Yes, I'll call it an understanding."

"I don't know what you're talking about," Rice snapped, but his tone lacked conviction. I sensed that Guy Thomas' seemingly wild suspicions had some basis in fact. I pursued my advantage.

"Of course," I said, "if I were taken into your confidence, I wouldn't dream of violating it by telling any tales out of school. But since you choose to distrust me, I am at liberty to act as I see fit."

Slowly a grin spread over Rice's florid features, and his blue eyes twinkled. He waved a hand, as if in defeat.

"Well, all right," he gestured. "I suppose I should have told you in the first place. But mind you, this is in the strictest confidence. I've got your word of honor you won't repeat a word?"

I indicated that he had.

"After all," he continued, "you acted square enough about quitting your job rather than letting poor Dora go ahead with it. It's only due you that I tell you the truth. You see, we were right up against it. Dora's the finest woman in the world, and I'm proud to know her. But every now and then she gets obstinate. And just because her kids don't like Thomas, and I don't like him, and you don't like him, she gets it into her head that there's a conspiracy against the poor boy. She thinks there's something fine in him that nobody else can see. Well, I knew what was coming. When she sprang the news, it was no news to me, and it was no news to Henry. So we decided on that cheap trick. Oh, I know it was cheap. But that's the sort of thing that makes an impression on Dora, if you know what I mean.

"She should have been an actress. She likes to do the ordinary things in a big, exciting way. And we figured—well, to be frank, I did, because Henry didn't want to scare his mother—fine boy, Henry—we figured that if she could get the idea that she's sacrificing her big love for her children, she'd be more excited about that than marrying this damn fool she's toting around. And I was right." There was a touch of pride in his voice.

"She's down with Henry now, and she can't do enough for him. So—there's the whole story and I'm glad I told you, and I know from my experience with the newspaper boys that it's safe in your keeping." He rose. "Any questions?" He smiled disarmingly and his eyes which could be agate were merry and frank. I shook my head. "Glad I told you," he said in parting. "You newspaper fellows find out everything if you're told or not. Hanged if I see how you do it!"

I could not tell him that all credit was due Mr. Thomas, and not me. Then I realized in surprise that the actor was perhaps not quite as vacuous as I imagined. Or perhaps he was super-sensitive to events that concerned his own welfare.

No one appeared at dinner save myself, and I dined in solitary state. Apparently even Mr. Thomas had deserted me. So, after dinner, I strolled out on deck. There was but a faint moon, and the sky was starless, but the night was warm and the southern waters placid. I breathed deeply, and having caught the first harbinger of the gentle climate, bitterly regretted the necessity of returning to riveting machines and dust-laden pavements.

As I passed the windows of the row of cabins on the starboard deck, I gathered that dinner was still in progress in Mrs. Breese's sitting-room. I could hear her voice, and that of her son. And occasionally Rice's hearty voice boomed forth. I moved on. Just as I reached the last window, I was attracted by a movement within the dark cabin. Sometimes, the faint stirring of the shadow of a leaf will rivet your attention. It was so in this case. I could not for the life of me tell you what made me stop at that moment and peer within the cabin.

And then I descried a vague figure, and as I strained to see I could recognize Guy Thomas. He was bent over a suitcase and rummaging through its contents with feverish haste.

"Now what in the world," I thought to myself, "is Guy Thomas doing in that boy's cabin?" To all outward appearances, the actor seemed to be engaged in some amateur burgling. But this I dismissed rightly as absurd. I moved cautiously and attempted to get a better view.

But Thomas had risen. Hastily he shut the suitcase, stopped to listen intently and then darted out of the room. I heard his footsteps in the corridor. He was headed for the deck. Instinctively I moved into the shadow of the bridge, and I saw Thomas advance in my direction. Then he stopped, directly in the glow of light that came from the corridor.

From his pocket he took a bulky object. I could not see it at first, and I was afraid to move closer. Then, as he held it in the light, I started. It was a pearl-handled revolver that he clutched in his hand, and with expert fingers I saw him click the cartridges from the barrel. These he hurled into the sea, and it seemed to me he heaved a sigh of relief. Then he put the revolver in his pocket, looked about once more to make sure he had not been discovered, and moved into the corridor again.

CHAPTER IV
ENTER THE RUSSIAN

THE *MARY ROSE* STEAMED past Morro Castle into Havana harbor.

Just before we landed, Mrs. Breese took me aside and mournfully complained that Mr. Rice and Henry had both decided that the press-agent must go.

"What can I do?" she moaned. "Henry will do the most desperate things if I cross him."

I assured her that my resignation was sincere and that she needn't trouble herself on my account. And, of course, she swore me to secrecy on all events transpiring on the yacht.

After the necessary customs and immigration formalities had been observed, we were permitted to go ashore. I was the first of the passengers off, and I felt a curious relief in being on my own again. I clambered into a decrepit taxi and was whirled to my hotel. Mrs. Breese, her children and Rice were going to the winter palace her former husband had built several years ago in the Vedado. I presumed Guy Thomas would be shipped to some hotel, and then, like myself, cast off into the cold world.

To the noisiest and most cosmopolitan of hotels my driver brought me, and as soon as I was settled, I plunged forth to see the town. Before I knew it, I found myself on the marble-studded Prado where the lamps shine as green satin through the trees. I walked leisurely down this most delightful of promenades, watching the fascinating mixtures of browns, blacks and olive-whites who shuffled past me.

I repulsed a dozen miserable Chinese vendors of peanuts, successfully negotiated two optimistic guides who leered promises of night life, paused to listen to the army band struggling with "La Bohème," and then found myself at the Prado Bar.

Now, the Prado Bar is the meeting place of the adventurers of the South, so it is not strange that it was here I was destined to see this evening the two men who were to be added to my cast of principals in the tragedy. It may have been a coincidence that Ben Smith was there. But I am inclined to believe that the

Russian deliberately chose the scene. I refuse to take his assurance that our meeting was entirely accidental. But I am anticipating my story.

After my experience of the yacht, I took the Prado Bar to my bosom as one would a long-lost friend. Do not misunderstand me. The friendship was not at all alcoholic. There were no thirsty Americans clamoring for hard liquors. The Prado Bar is too far from the center of town, just around the corner from the battered Malecon where at night angry waters swirl over the sea wall and splash the proud boulevard.

I found the tumult of the waters pleasant music; the bartenders were polite and capable; the bacardi genuine and cheap. And Pancho, the proprietor, with his swarthy face framed in the radiance of his thousand bottles gleaming from the highly polished shelves, hospitably bade me welcome. There were few in the bar at the moment, but they looked my own kind—genteel wanderers, known commonly as tropical tramps. I was about to open conversational negotiations with two likely-looking prospects when someone called my name, and I whirled about to find myself face to face with Ben Smith.

"Of all people!" I welcomed him.

"The same to you!" And we shook hands warmly. I had not seen Ben Smith in three years.

He had been attached to Police Headquarters in Richmond when I covered that institution for the Star. He was responsible for the solution of the Stephenson murder—that strange crime where after many months of inquiry Smith finally discovered that the wealthy bachelor had been done to death by his own brother, one of Richmond's wealthiest and most respectable citizens. You undoubtedly recall the case, for its ramifications were spread upon the newspapers of the world. Smith gained considerable recognition as a result of this coup, and when the Cuban police created an American department for the benefit of our crooks who wandered down there, Smith was loaned to head the department.

We had become good friends in Richmond, despite the detective's suspicion of everything that tended to make life and his profession romantic. This tendency of his spoiled many a good story. Nevertheless, I was very glad to see him now.

He had not changed much. Smith never did look the usual police detective so easily ridiculed upon the stage. He was given to shell-rimmed glasses, an impassive though kindly face, and he always impressed you at first sight as a humdrum mediocrity. In any crowd he was just the average man. In Havana, with flannels, panama and a deep coat of tan, he seemed the typical tourist.

He wanted to know my immediate purpose in life, and I told him of my experience with Mrs. Breese. He listened carefully. When I was done, he said:

"That's very funny, because I was just talking about the lady this morning with—well, I never will remember his name. He's a Russian." Smith chuckled. "Strange duck! But I kind of like him. He's going to meet me here later and I'll introduce him to you."

"Who is he?" I demanded.

"Well," drawled Smith, "aside from the fact that I can't remember his name, he showed me papers which prove that before the revolution he was a big gun with the Czarist police. He'll tell you all about himself the first five minutes. He's not exactly modest. How much there is to him, I don't know. He came into my office one day and said he had a mission. It seems he'd been working on some murder in Riga just before the revolution broke, and he was right on the track of it when the Bolsheviks threw him out. He seems to have enough money and time, and he's still working on the case long distance. For some reason or other, he's particularly interested in Mrs. Breese."

"But why?"

Smith shrugged his shoulders. "He won't tell me. He asked me to see if I couldn't place him on our staff. He wasn't interested in salary. Just wanted the job. Of course, I couldn't. I promised I'd talk it over with the chief. But I knew it was no use. We didn't know the man and we haven't got room for him if we did." Smith suddenly whispered out of the corner of his mouth: "Here he is now."

I observed a tall and well-made individual striding up to us. A giant in stature, he was an imposing sight and a remarkable contrast to Smith. This man would be distinguishable in any crowd, with his barrel chest, enormous shoulders, his massive face, ornamented by a proud and well-combed mustache of the Russian school, from which peered small blue eyes. He was impeccably dressed in flashing white linen, and as he walked he swung a heavy silver-headed cane as if it were a swagger stick.

"Hello, there," Smith said. "I've talked it over with them but they can't see it. Sorry!"

The big man bowed.

"Thank you. I did not expect otherwise." His words were clipped, military. "I deeply appreciate your efforts."

Smith introduced us.

"This is a newspaper friend of mine, Mr. Abbott," he turned to the Russian apologetically. "I forget your name. I'm sorry. I was never much good on Russian names."

"Boris Sergeivitch Perutkin, formerly of the Russian Secret Police," the big man prompted, and bowed. "So you are a newspaper man. I am indeed pleased to meet you."

Smith looked at his watch.

"I've got a date downtown," he said. "But I'll be back in an hour. By the way,"—he turned to the Russian. "Mr. Abbott here has just come down from New York with the Breese family. Maybe he can tell you what you want to know."

The Russian's little blue eyes were trained on me.

"So! That is very interesting. You must join me in a glass."

"And," Smith continued, "you'll find that Mr. Abbott can be trusted. I've known him a long time."

"I am sure of Mr. Abbott," the Russian bowed politely, as Smith left us. Then he turned to the bartender: "*Cordon rouge*—the same as I had last night." He turned back to me. "Do you mind champagne? I drink nothing else."

We seated ourselves in a corner far from the other patrons of the bar, and soon the glasses with yellow magic were before us. The Russian sipped his drink slowly, with the air of a connoisseur. He did not at once ask anything of Mrs. Breese, but instead discussed far-flung topics from American politics to horses. I had an uneasy feeling that he was testing me. He seemed anxious to know everything that had happened to me since I was a child in swaddling clothes. Then, suddenly, his adroit questioning ceased, and he told me about himself.

"I am that anomaly," he smiled, "a detective without a country. But I have a case—a very peculiar case. I have devoted six years to its solution, and I am still far from it. Mr. Smith says you can be trusted. I am going to tell you about that case, because you may be of great help to me. You know Mrs. Breese well?"

I said I knew her fairly well, but that I was no longer connected with her household.

"That does not matter," he responded. "The difficulty hitherto has been that I could not legitimately gain access to the most important circle in my case. I conceive of my case as a series of circles, criss-crossing each other. In one of these circles my case is as plain as a photograph. I have not yet reached that circle. Perhaps you can help me."

My face showed I was puzzled. He laughed. "Of course, you do not understand me. Let me put it this way. Who were your fellow-passengers on the yacht?"

I enumerated them: Mrs. Breese, her two children, Gordon Rice and Guy Thomas.

"Excellent!" murmured the Russian. "There is only one absent. Six years ago, Mr. Abbott, Mrs. Breese, her two children, Gordon Rice and Guy Thomas were in Riga. But Mr. Breese was there, too. He is the only one absent."

"But I don't see the significance," I protested.

"Six years ago, in Riga, a very strange crime occurred which directly affected Mrs. Breese. A man was murdered. His murderer was never found. Do you see the significance now?"

"A murder affecting Mrs. Breese?" I indicated my scepticism. "I never heard a word of it."

"There was never a word printed," the Russian said. "Providence seemed to intervene on behalf of the criminal at the very moment that I thought the case would be solved. The murderer escaped. And yet I know, as surely as I know anything, one of your fellow-passengers on that yacht is the murderer."

His sharp little eyes, almost hypnotic in their power, blazed angrily.

"There is no punishment for him—or her—now. My government is no more. But an innocent man walks with the shadow of suspicion upon him." I quote the Russian's exact words. "This man's life-happiness has been taken away from him because of that crime. And if I cannot punish the murderer, I can at least help an innocent victim to re-establish himself. I can at least right a great wrong."

CHAPTER V
THE LAST OF THE CIRCLE

I SHALL REPEAT here the story the Russian told me. I made notes of it later in my hotel room, and the facts are exact. In the summer of 1918, Mary Rose Breese was married to the Count Giering-Trelovitch in Riga, Russia. She was then eighteen, and extraordinarily beautiful. Disillusionment had not yet written boredom into her fragile features. The Count was twenty-five.

Unlike most unions of this kind, no sordid motives marred their relationship. The Count was handsome, witty, a brave soldier and sportsman. His estates were flourishing. He insisted he would accept no dowry. He had met Mary Rose Breese during a visit to America and theirs had been a story-book romance. The Russian laid great emphasis upon this point. "It was enough to make you cry tears of pleasure," he exclaimed with Slavic sentimentality. "Just to see them together. In these days such romances are so rare!"

The marriage ceremony took place in the Giering-Trelovitch castle. There was the quality of a bygone age in the preparations for this festive event. From all parts of Europe friends of the Count poured into Riga. The Count kept open house, and when he could no longer accommodate the thousands of guests, local mansions and even cottages were requisitioned. The Count's peasants toiled and feasted with their master.

Several days before the ceremony, Mr. and Mrs. Breese arrived with the bride, and Henry, then a youth of fifteen. Mrs. Breese, of course, was proud to be the prospective mother-in-law of a Count, which somehow offset the sad fact that possession of a married daughter would officially end that youth to which she clung so tenaciously.

The moment she arrived, she took charge of matters in characteristic fashion. The Count was too happy to interfere. Mr. Breese was not so pleased at events. He said he'd prefer to have an American for a son-in-law, but he had been too preoccupied to venture any but the mildest objections.

Mr. Breese received a wire from a business associate, Gordon Rice, several days before the ceremony. An important transaction with some French industrialists was in progress, and Rice requested Mr. Breese's presence in Paris. Realizing he could not desert his daughter at her wedding, he telegraphed

Rice, inviting him to the ceremony, suggesting they could discuss the matter in Riga. Rice arrived, which accounts for his presence in the former Russian city.

At that time, Guy Thomas had known Mrs. Breese only casually. She had met him several months before. He had come to Paris as gigolo to a harmless old lady who wanted to see the sights. But the harmless old lady discarded him in favor of a native guide, and Thomas was left without funds. He was struck with an inspiration and wired Mrs. Breese of his desire to be of assistance to her. Mrs. Breese, reflecting that she would be alone in Paris for several weeks after the ceremony, promptly hired him as her temporary social secretary—and Guy Thomas hurried to the feast.

Upon consulting my notes, I find that the name of the man who was murdered was the Baron Peter Setovski, whose estates adjoined those of the Count Giering-Trelovitch. The murder took place two days after the marriage ceremony. The Baron Peter Setovski was not a guest at the wedding. He was the one man the Count had not invited. It was brought out later that the two men had quarrelled shortly before the wedding on some trivial boundary dispute, and the Count, who was hot-headed and impulsive, broke off all relations with his neighbor.

The murder had taken place in the Baron's bedroom, about midnight, two days after the lavish wedding ceremony which is still recalled in Riga for its prodigal splendor. The Baron was found slumped upon the floor of his bedroom, shot through the heart. None of the numerous servants had heard the shot.

The only visitor the Baron had received that night was the Count Giering-Trelovitch. Examined by the police, the Count said that he had gone to his neighbor offering reconciliation. The Count could not explain satisfactorily why he had chosen the hour of midnight for such a mission except that he always did things impulsively. He said he had been so profoundly happy that the quarrel with his neighbor disturbed him, and when everyone had gone to bed he had ridden over to the Baron's estate to see him. He said that the breach had been healed, the Baron had drunk a glass of vodka with him in friendship, and he, the Count, had returned to his home and his bride.

Although the police were reluctant to arrest the young nobleman, they were compelled to warn him not to leave the country. Detectives insisted upon prowling about the estate, and what had once been the scene of unrestrained festivity became the laboratory of a crime.

Of course, the Countess at first refused to believe a word against her husband, despite the damning circumstantial evidence. Mrs. Breese and Mr. Breese, however, were for once united in the opinion that it was distinctly up to the bridegroom to clear himself. It was at this time that the Russian detective was summoned to help unravel the mystery.

After a lengthy talk with the Count, my informant was convinced that the solution of the murder lay elsewhere. He promptly set to work.

But shortly after he arrived, Mrs. Breese insisted she must go home, and suggested her daughter go with her. Mary Rose Breese, now the Countess Giering-Trelovitch, fell in with the plan, for the atmosphere of suspicion and hostility that followed the murder of the Baron was hardly in keeping with the glorious honeymoon she had pictured to herself. But she did not want to leave the Count behind, and suggested he come with them. Unfortunately, he had not told her he was practically under house arrest, and when this confession was extorted from him, she was horrified.

Then, events beyond the power of Mrs. Breese intervened. The Russian revolution, long smouldering, now blazed in full force, and reached even Riga, long after it was an accomplished fact in Petrograd. The local police were ousted, and the murder of the Baron was swallowed in the explosion. The Count fled with the Breese ménage to Paris.

But if the Count was no longer in danger from official prosecution, suspicion still clung to him. He noted in despair that his bride became more and more reluctant to meet him. Matters were not helped when his estates were confiscated and he was left a pittance. Now his position was difficult indeed.

One morning Mrs. Breese, in her high-handed fashion, announced that she was sailing for America in a few days. Her daughter, she said, would accompany her. The meaning of this was perfectly clear to the Count. Heart-broken, despondent at his reverses, he stolidly consented to a divorce.

"I myself was in Paris then," the Russian said. "I, too, had to flee, for although I am not a Czarist in spirit, my connection with the police damned me in the eyes of the revolutionists. Naturally, I spent a good deal of time with the Count, for I had grown to like him very, very much.

"I remember he asked me to go to the railroad station with him to see them off, for the divorce was to be gotten quietly and the proprieties were to be observed. Mrs. Breese was very insistent upon that. I notice that in her own case she was not so discreet. However, as I say, we went to say good-bye at the Gare du Nord. Mrs. Breese treated the Count very coldly. She seemed to be finished with him forever, and her manner indicated as much. Mr. Breese, too, didn't make matters particularly pleasant.

"But the Countess was affected, despite her pose. I could see that. I suspected that she had cried many nights when she was alone, and I was sure, too, that if it had not been for her mother, who dominated her, she would never have lost faith in my friend. But what will you? Some people are born to dominate, and others to be dominated. I could see that the girl was putty in her mother's hands, and the Count realized that, too. It was tragic, for their romance had been beautiful.

"When they left finally, the Count was so melancholy that I was afraid he would do something foolish. I did my best to cheer him up. Finally I said, for my reputation was at stake, that despite the extraordinary difficulties of the case, I would do my best to clear his name. And then, I assured him, his bride would receive him to her arms again. Of course, I didn't tell him that in my opinion Mrs. Breese had cast him off as a son-in-law not because he was under suspicion, but because he had become a poor man.

"Fortunately, the Count had rescued some family jewels, and I had some small investments in London. We had enough to live on and to travel in a modest way. The Count acquired the hobby of etchings from his father, and I encouraged him to visit the museums and to keep his mind occupied. We wandered around Europe, and had a fairly pleasant time. Then, because the Count insisted, we went to America.

"We had both been reading the newspapers assiduously. The one thing that kept the Count buoyant was the fact that his bride never remarried. But when he tried to see her, she refused to meet him—at the insistence, I think, of her mother. Even during the trial, when the Count thought he could be of at least moral support to his wife, she consistently avoided him. Once they met, but the Countess did not say a word, and wouldn't listen to him.

"When we read in the newspapers that they were coming here, nothing I could say would dissuade the Count from coming here, too. And then, after thinking out the case, I reached the conclusion that perhaps it was wise. For, by a strange coincidence, these very people, with the exception of Mr. Breese, were present at the time of the murder of the Baron Peter Setovski. And I feel that I have never been nearer to a solution. Tell me——"

The Russian plied me with questions, some of them so minute and trivial that I could not attach any importance to them. I must recite all the events of the trial, all the testimony. I recounted some of the adventures of the yacht, although I did not feel free to tell of the escapade of the Breese boy.

Then he insisted that I come with him at once to his flat to meet his friend, the Count Giering-Trelovitch. Although the hour was late I could not refuse, for I felt strangely drawn to this unfortunate young man whose story he had told me. I discovered that the two Russians shared a tiny apartment on the Malecon. The Count himself had just returned from a lonely promenade, he said. The morning newspaper was under his arm.

"This gentleman," the detective presented me, "has come down with Mrs. Breese and her family on the yacht. He has seen your wife."

The Count, who was prepared to be formally polite, now wrung my hand with embarrassing cordiality.

"That is the best news I have heard in many years!" he exclaimed, his rather melancholy blue eyes lighting up. "How is she? Is she well? Is she happy? What did she say? How does she look?"

There was an engaging boyish impulsiveness about his manner now that quite won me. I could see now what the detective meant when he said that the Count's wedding was a story-book romance. If the Princes that walk the earth are paunchy, given to gout and short-temper, this young man defied nature and upheld art at least pictorially. Blond, finely featured, slender and graceful of carriage, he had been designed to blend with the fragile loveliness of Mary Rose Breese.

"What did she wear? She dressed so exquisitely always." For the life of me, I could not tell him. He seemed disappointed, baffled. "But what did she say? Didn't she say anything?"

I explained that I had but little opportunity to talk with her. But I said she seemed well and, as far as I could tell, happy.

He sighed, as if relieved. "I have been trying to see her. Boris Sergeivitch has undoubtedly told you my story. I feel she needs me, but what can I do? If you could get a message to her——"

But here I was called upon to explain that my relations with the Breese family had been severed. He seemed downcast.

"If I felt," he said, "that she really didn't want to see me, I would disappear and she would never hear a word from me. But it's her mother who's back of this. I know! That woman!" He seemed to sink in a brown study. "She should be punished."

The detective had apparently been paying little attention to his friend. He had picked up the morning paper—the morning edition of the Havana Post, and was reading its spare columns with absorbed interest. Suddenly he whistled, as if in surprise. I turned to him. The Count, too, looked up.

"Read this," the detective commanded, pointing with a stubby forefinger to a paragraph noting the American visitors to the city.

It was recorded here that Mr. Henry Breese, Sr., had arrived by airplane from Miami and was stopping at the Sevilla-Biltmore. I re-read the paragraph to make sure my eyes had not deceived me. I wondered, amazed, what motive could prompt the elderly Breese to come to the city to which his divorced wife had fled.

"Interesting!" the Russian exclaimed, and then to the Count: "Read this, my friend." The young man took the newspaper from him and examined it. "It is now complete!"

I looked blank. The Count peered down at him, puzzled.

"The last of the circle is here!" the detective continued meditatively. "The absent one has arrived!"

CHAPTER VI
MURDER

AWEEK PASSED, VERY PLEASANTLY for me, and during this time I paid but scant attention to the Breese ménage. The Russian seemed to have disappeared, and Ben Smith was busy with a case that involved the extradition of an absconded bank teller. Left to my own resources, I explored the town, sampled the native Morro crabs (as delicious as our own lobsters), sipped gentle Spanish wines and watched the shimmying Rumba dancers in the lower music-halls.

It was inevitable that I meet various members of the permanent American colony in my wanderings, and I soon discovered that Mrs. Breese had already made her presence felt. Just what her divorced husband was doing in the city no one seemed to know. Certainly he was not seen at the home he had built, and if, as presumed, he had journeyed down for reconciliation his efforts evidently had been in vain. Mrs. Breese entertained discreetly, and it was common gossip that Guy Thomas was with her constantly. If Mrs. Breese had renounced the actor after her son's toying with suicide, she had apparently restored him to favor now. It was the general impression that Mr. Thomas was the lady's fiancé.

Just about this time I first heard the words: "The Gilded Cage". Who it was who so dubbed the Breese palace I do not know. Probably it was some malicious wit. Undoubtedly the name rose from Guy Thomas' peculiar status in the household, for those of the colony that I met were busy laughing at Mr. Thomas as the bird in the gilded cage, and momentarily expecting formal announcement of the engagement of the wealthy woman to the idler many years her junior.

Then, one evening, while I was at dinner, Ben Smith wandered into the dining-room of my hotel and joined me in black coffee and liqueurs. He seemed preoccupied, and I knew that he had sought me out for a purpose. Finally he said: "How well do you know old man Breese?"

I said I had seen him frequently during the trial, but had not exchanged a dozen words with him. Outwardly, he struck me as the type of short-tempered executive who would be a terror to his employees and so much wax in the modelling hands of Mrs. Breese. I asked Smith the reason for his inquiry.

"Well," he said finally, "very funny thing happened. Last night old Breese called up and said he wanted to see me at his hotel—the Sevilla-Biltmore. Had something tremendously important and confidential. Hinted that it would be worth my while. I couldn't make head or tail of it, but I promised I'd be over to see him."

"I wonder if anything's happened," I speculated. "What reason has he got to go to the police? And what did he mean by 'worth your while'?"

"I don't know," Smith confessed. "I couldn't very well question him over the phone. I'm repeating to you all he said to me. I don't even know how he got hold of my name. He never met me, and, as far as I know, never even heard of me." Smith took out his cheap nickel-plated watch which he seemed to treasure above all earthly possessions. "I've got a date to see him in five minutes. Want to come over?"

"I'll be glad to," I said, "but I may be in the way."

"That's all right," Smith assured me. "I kind of feel that I may need a witness, and I certainly need someone who knows the inside of that Breese family. Leave it to me."

It was only a short walk from my unpretentious hotel to the palatial Sevilla-Biltmore. Smith announced himself, and the elevator swept us up to the seventh story and the most splendid of suites. Mr. Breese greeted Smith cordially, but looked askance at me. Although I had seen him scores of times during the trial, he apparently had not recognized me, and Smith airily presented me as his assistant.

Breese hesitated for a moment, then apparently decided to accept my presence. He asked us to make ourselves comfortable, and submitted a box of Partagas, a decanter of whiskey, a siphon and a bowl of ice. He seemed laboring hard to create an atmosphere of friendly good-will before he plunged into the business at hand. We chatted for a while of nothing in particular. Finally, lighting a cigar slowly, and glancing at Smith from under bristling grey eyebrows, he said: "I suppose you wonder why I called you."

"Yes," Smith acknowledged, "you sounded kind of queer over the phone."

"I suppose I must have," he smiled wrily. "I've been under a tremendous strain, let me tell you!" He gulped his whiskey and soda, and cleared his throat. "I don't know exactly how to begin. I suppose the best thing I can do is to come right down to the heart of the problem. Let me ask you, Mr. Smith: Isn't it a fact that it is a duty of the police to prevent crimes as well as punish the criminals?"

Smith looked blank.

"Why, sure," he said finally. "Whenever we can we do try to prevent them."

"Very well, then. I know of a crime that is being contemplated at this very moment. What ought I to do?"

"What kind of a crime?"

Breese fixed the detective with his rather sharp eyes.

"You know my position, Mr. Smith. You know my standing. You know I wouldn't give false information. You know I'm a man of means."

Smith nodded.

"Suppose I were to tell you that at this minute a murder is being planned—what could you do?"

"That's a hard one," said Smith, but he was sitting erect and tense. "Don't you think you'd better be more explicit?"

Breese nodded. "I'll put all my cards on the table, Mr. Smith. I've got to, although there are certain things I'd rather not talk about. I suppose you know that my wife divorced me recently. I came down here—well, I thought I was hasty, inconsiderate. I was willing to make amends, do anything to save my family. Even if I weren't fond of my wife, I'm crazy enough about my children to do anything. I came down here for a reconciliation. When I got here, my wife wouldn't see me. My children wouldn't see me."

He paused, swallowing, as if this bitter pill were more than he could bear. Smith made no comment.

"I discovered my wife contemplated marrying this actor, Guy Thomas. Since my wife wouldn't permit me to talk to her, I did my best to get word to her. But no use. She can be very headstrong, as anyone who knows her will tell you. Well, I was just about ready to go back, licked, when through certain sources I needn't disclose to you, I learned that my wife was making a will. Now remember this—for it's very important. She is making—probably has made it by now—a will leaving her entire fortune to Guy Thomas.

"Shortly after I learned this, I put certain detectives to work in New York to discover facts about this young man. I felt if I could expose him to Dora she would see the light. Well, I did get some facts about the young man, in a cable today. Mr. Thomas has a certain young lady in New York waiting for him. She got word from him two days ago to be prepared to sail for Europe."

Ben Smith listened attentively as the old man continued:

"That isn't all. I went to see Mrs. Breese, and waited in the reception-room for her. While I waited, I heard Mr. Thomas on the telephone, talking to New York. I heard him say: 'For God's sake, wait, can't you. I'm going to make a lot of money soon.' That's all I heard because Mrs. Breese sent out word that she would not receive me and I had to go.

"Now, gentlemen, as sure as I'm sitting here I know that Guy Thomas is preparing to do away with Mrs. Breese!" He had risen in his excitement. "I know that he influenced her to make out this will. I'm not easily frightened. I'm sane. I'm a practical man of business. I know it sounds wild, but——"

The telephone buzzed softly. Annoyed, impatient, Mr. Breese picked it up. "Yes, who is it?"

Then——

"Good God, man!" I saw him grow deathly white. The telephone fell from his limp hands. He tottered for a moment, and then steadied himself against a chair.

"Mrs. Breese has—has—just been found dead!"

CHAPTER VII
INQUIRY

SMITH AND I LITERALLY threw ourselves into a taxi, and raced to the Gilded Cage. Breese had said he had not the strength to accompany us, and after looking at his ashen face I could readily believe him.

Our cab whirled past the grilled windows and stone fronts of the dark houses. The air was heavy with the perfume of a tropical night. The streets were practically deserted. Only an occasional hotel flared brilliantly as we raced by.

Before I was quite aware of it, our driver had turned into Calle L and then stopped with a screeching of brakes, in the manner of Latin chauffeurs. The Gilded Cage was an imposing sight, beautifully white, with enormous marble pillars, huge mahogany doors, massive grilles to delight the heart of any lover of cunning ironwork, and a magnificent garden studded with royal palms that kept the vulgar street far from the inmates of the palace.

As I came up the stairs to the terrace, Smith always slightly ahead of me, I noted an exquisite sculptured fountain piece of six nudes bending over still black water and glistening white in the moonlight. The palace was still as death. Only a faint light seemed to filter through from the reception-hall. The rest of the house seemed steeled in darkness.

Smith pressed a tiny button set into a burnished gilt frame. A bell pealed softly within, and we heard footsteps. The huge door swung open, and an owlish-looking native policeman stared at us suspiciously, one hand at his revolver holster. But Smith displayed his credentials, and we were ushered in without further delay.

In the reception-room, Smith at once reached for the telephone and notified the Cuban Secret Police he had taken charge of the case and that he was now at the scene of the murder. While he talked, I looked about me, and even in the faint light I was impressed with the curious fact that every bit of furniture in the reception-room was gilt. I noted particularly a fine Spanish clock of impressive proportions, with hands and case gaudily inlaid with gold; a full sweep of gold brocade curtains upon the French windows; and a great hall mirror likewise decorated.

Smith informed me that his superiors had approved his handling of the case, and that a medical examiner would be despatched forthwith. The native policeman had arrived just a few moments before we did. Without further instruction on Smith's part, he led us through a curtained door into the drawing-room.

The room measured about thirty-five feet by forty, and about twenty feet in height. The floor was of gaily colored tile, the walls and ceiling panelled in rich mahogany. There were two enormous French windows leading to the garden, four by ten feet. One door led to the reception-room. Another door took us to the library.

I am setting forth these facts from my notes. My first impression was too jumbled to permit such blunt recording. For a figure lay outstretched in one corner, and I still have in my memory a confused picture of diamond buckles and silk stockings, blue velvet and green emeralds, a shock of blond hair and stiff bejewelled fingers. As we came nearer, I noted, shivering, that the floor tiles near her were a bright red.

This was Mrs. Breese in her last moment of life. She could not have chosen a more sensational exit. I could not believe that this vital, domineering woman had been transformed into the still and gory heap before me. Her eyes as they were that moment still haunt me. There was such a ghastly look of surprise in those set eyes of hers. Possibly it was a physical distortion born of her last moment of suffering.

Smith bent over the prone figure. "Right through the heart," he said finally. "Don't need any of these native medical examiners to tell me she died immediately."

Then he addressed the policeman in Spanish and inquired: "Where are the members of the family?"

"They are upstairs. Shall I call them?"

"No. Not yet. I want to take a look around first."

He went to the two French windows and noted that both were locked securely from the inside.

Consulting my notes once more, I find that the body was exactly four feet from the left wall. I jotted down every item of furniture in this room. There were the following major pieces: a hand-carved table in the center, with four chairs; eight huge tapestried chairs against the wall; a bulky secretary; a Spanish marble mantel; an ornate and new radio in silver and black; a Jo Davidson bust of Mrs. Breese; two large canvases, one a Romney, the other, I believe, an Italian primitive; and several water colors and pastels of modernist persuasion. A veritable jumble of art.

Although we searched carefully, we found no weapon. There were no signs of violence in the room or upon the body. The furniture was not upset and the clothes of the woman were unruffled. Only that horrible look of surprise in her set eyes, which Smith, too, commented upon. It was not so much terror that was written there, it seemed to me, as it was sheer amazement at the tragedy that had overtaken her. I could readily believe that death was far from the thoughts of this woman.

"If only," I said, "there was something to that superstition that the eyes of the victim photograph the murderer in the last moment of life! We'd have the secret of this in twenty-four hours!"

Smith grunted impatiently, as if annoyed at such idle speculation. He prowled about the room, methodically noting a host of what seemed to me uninteresting detail. Finally he said: "There's one thing I've learned—there's no such thing as waste motion in a case of this kind. One must overlook nothing."

"And what have you found?" I demanded.

"One thing—and that the man who did this job——"

"Assuming it is a man," I intervened.

"Assuming it is a man," he repeated. "But whoever did this job left us a perfect piece of marksmanship. One bullet killed her, and as far as I can tell, it went straight through the heart. The medical examiner can check up on that." (Dr. Miguel de Cassandra later confirmed this fact.)

"May it not have been a stroke of luck—this perfect marksmanship?" I suggested.

Smith shook his head. "No. This job was done in a hurry. It had to be. The killer couldn't trust to luck." He turned to the policeman. "Where are the servants?"

For answer the policeman led us through the reception-room down a long corridor and into the servants' quarters. In the huge kitchen we found fully fifteen domestics huddled in whispering groups. There were five Jamaica blacks, two Japanese, one of them my scowling steward, several half-caste Cubans, a disdainful English butler who stood in solitary glory in a corner of his own, and a rotund and rosy-cheeked French chef who even now was ogling a pretty half-caste maid. At our entrance they all became silent.

Smith singled out the English butler for his first witness. His name was Rodney Brandlock. He was perhaps forty, rather thin, with watery blue eyes inclined to squint. He had been engaged only a few weeks ago by Mrs. Breese.

It developed that it was he who had discovered Mrs. Breese's body and had summoned the policeman from his post.

"Tell us exactly what happened," Smith commanded.

"After dinner," he began, "Mrs. Breese and Mr. Thomas adjourned to the drawing-room for coffee. The two children went immediately upstairs."

"What time was dinner?" Smith interrupted.

"Dinner tonight was at nine. We had no set hour. In any case, I brought coffee and liqueurs into the drawing-room. I returned about fifteen minutes later to remove the cups and glasses. Mrs. Breese and Mr. Thomas were chatting."

"About what?"

"I'm afraid I can't tell you. I didn't stop to listen." There was reproof in the servant's eyes. "In any case, I removed the tray and just as I did so, the telephone rang. I answered it.—It was for Mrs. Breese from Mr. Rice."

"Where was Mr. Rice?"

"I believe he was dining at the American Ministry. He wished to speak to Mrs. Breese. I gave the receiver to Mrs. Breese and went on my way down to the pantry. I happened to look at the clock at that time, and I noted it was exactly half-past ten. I thought of taking a walk for a bit of fresh air, and I returned to the drawing-room to ask Mrs. Breese if there would be anything further she wanted for the night. When I got in——"

"Go ahead!" Smith commanded.

"I—I found the room dark." The butler's voice was husky. "I—I couldn't understand that, but I put up the lights, and then I saw——" he swallowed. "So I ran upstairs and——"

"Yes——"

"I found Mr. Thomas in the corridor, and I told him. Then I ran out for a policeman. I guess that's all."

Smith nodded.

"You sent for a doctor?"

"—I didn't. I leaned over and saw that Mrs. Breese was dead, and Mr. Thomas didn't say anything. He seemed terribly shocked."

"But didn't it occur to you that you ought to send for a doctor?"

"Yes, I did think of it, but Mr. Thomas instructed me to fetch a policeman, and I did. And as I say, there was no question Mrs. Breese was dead. Then when I got back, the children were down, and it was out of my hands."

"So Mr. Thomas sent you for the policeman?" Smith asked.

"Yes."

"Did he run down to examine the body himself?"

"No, sir."

"What did he say exactly?"

"He said: 'Fetch the police!' Or: 'Get the police!' I think he said. That's all I know, sir. None of the servants know anything about it. I'm the only one."

"You heard no shot?"

"No, sir."

Smith turned to the motley group. "Did any of you hear a shot here tonight?" he demanded. They all shook their heads. He turned once more to the butler.

"When you returned with the policeman, where did you find Mr. Thomas?"

"He was still upstairs, sir."

"He hadn't come down?"

"No, sir. But the children were down."

"That'll be all," said Smith. "Will you go upstairs now and tell Mr. Thomas to come down to the drawing-room immediately?"

CHAPTER VIII
A CLEAR CASE

WHEN WE HAD DONE examining the servants, these were the undisputed facts that emerged: Mrs. Breese was last seen alive at about ten minutes after ten, and discovered dead at half-past ten. No shot was heard. There were fifteen servants in the house at the time, Mr. Thomas, the Countess and young Henry Breese. No visitors had called during the evening. This fact was confirmed by the butler and by the Japanese footman who answered the bell. There had, in fact, been no visitors at all during the day.

We returned to the drawing-room to find Mr. Thomas awaiting us. I could not at first recognize him. His hair was dishevelled, his eyes bloodshot.

"My name's Smith, I'm with the police here. I just want to ask you a few questions, Mr. Thomas."

Thomas did not seem to hear him. His eyes were fixed upon the outstretched figure of Mrs. Breese.

"What do you want to know?" he managed to say finally. His hands were trembling visibly.

"Now take it easy," Smith placated him. "I know this must be a terrible shock to you, and I don't want to make it any harder. This is just a matter of routine."

Thomas looked up quickly, with relief, I thought. He breathed easier.

"I don't know a thing—not a thing," he assured us.

"As I understand it," began Smith, "you and Mrs. Breese were alone in this room after dinner. Mrs. Breese received a telephone call from Mr. Rice. What happened then, Mr. Thomas?"

"Why—nothing happened. I went upstairs while she was talking to Rice—I went upstairs to write a letter. Just when I'd gotten through, the butler ran up to tell me what had happened. It was an awful blow to me. I can't realize yet it's true." He stared as if fascinated at the outstretched body.

"You heard no sound upstairs?"

"No—nothing."

"When the butler ran up to tell you the news, what did you do?"

"Why—I sent him to fetch a policeman at once!"

"You didn't think a doctor was necessary?"

"No. He said she was—dead."

"He may have been excited. Surely you went down to investigate."

Thomas squirmed.

"No—I didn't. I couldn't—I couldn't go in that room alone. My nerves wouldn't stand it."

Smith made careful notes of his answers. He was about to proceed when the door bell pealed. The native policeman returned with Gordon Rice. The promoter stamped into the room and then stopped short at the sight of the body. His eyes were red with rage as he swung at Thomas.

"Well, what have you got to say for yourself?" he barked.

"What have I——?"

"Yes!" Rice shouted. "Don't stand there pretending innocence! You're not that good an actor!"

"Just a minute," intervened Smith. "I'm conducting this inquiry."

"Then it's high time you knew the facts," snapped Rice. He turned to us. "I always knew this man was a weakling and a rotter, but I didn't think he was a murderer."

"I say, I say!" the actor stammered in his fright. His face was white.

"You accuse this man of killing Mrs. Breese?" Smith demanded.

"Yes, I do!"

Now the actor looked from one to the other of us like a stricken animal. He tried to say something, but couldn't.

"On what ground?"

"Here are the facts, if you want them."

"I want them very much," Smith said.

"Look here——" interrupted the actor.

"You'll have every opportunity," Smith assured him, "to make any answer you want." The actor slumped into a chair, keeping his eyes fixed now upon Rice, watching his every move.

"I've just been to see Mr. Breese," Rice began.

"As you may know, I was Mrs. Breese's business adviser and friend. I'm frank to say I never liked this man personally. I strenuously objected when Mrs. Breese said she proposed marrying him. However, I'm fair enough, I think, not to make any accusation on prejudice. I've got facts! And I want to present them right to his face. I don't do anything underhanded." The actor had risen and drawn nearer. Rice reached into his pocket and produced a sheaf of telegrams.

"About a week ago, Mr. Breese came to me. We hadn't been on very good terms since the trial, but we buried the hatchet. I told Breese to make every effort to patch things up. I felt, just as he did, that it would be a calamity for Mrs. Breese to marry this man. Breese asked me what to do. Of course, we never suspected anything like this!" He shook his head. "It's a wonder to me I can still think straight. I've never had a shock like this before. Well—I advised Breese to wire a certain detective agency, the Burns people, and get all the facts on this young man. We thought if we had the facts, Dora—Mrs. Breese—would see things straight. And since we knew we were playing against time, the agency was instructed to wire us the minute they got anything. Well, they got plenty. Look at this!"

Without further comment, Rice extended the following telegrams. I reproduce them herewith:

HENRY BREESE
SEVILLA BILTMORE
HAVANA

ACTING YOUR INSTRUCTIONS YOUR PARTY (GUY THOMAS) RESIDES THREE FORTY FIVE WEST FORTY FIFTH STREET STOP FLAT NOW OCCUPIED BY MISS BELINDA SAUNDERS CHORUS GIRL STOP MISS SAUNDERS DESCRIBES SELF AS PARTYS FIANCEE STOP AGENT THIRTY SIX ENGAGING MISS SAUNDERS IN CONVERSATION LEARNED YOUR PARTY WIRED MISS SAUNDERS TO BE PREPARED SAIL FOR GRAND TOUR EUROPE SOON STOP

WILLIAMS

HENRY BREESE
SEVILLA BILTMORE
HAVANA
YOUR PARTY WAS PHONED BY MISS SAUNDERS AND INFORMED SHE WAS READY TO DEPART EUROPE STOP YOUR PARTY SAID DELAY HAD ARISEN STOP MISS SAUNDERS PROVOKED SAID WOULDNT DELAY STOP YOUR PARTY INFORMED HER HE WOULD HAVE LOTS OF MONEY IF SHED WAIT STOP MISS SAUNDERS THREATENED SUE BREACH OF PROMISE ON RUMOUR REACHING NEW YORK YOUR PARTY ABOUT TO MARRY WEALTHY WOMAN STOP WIRING FURTHER

  WILLIAMS

          HENRY BREESE
          SEVILLA BILTMORE
          HAVANA
          YOUR PARTY SENT WIRE MISS SAUNDERS BE PREPARED
          LEAVE IMMEDIATELY STOP WILL MEET HER PARIS STOP
                                                    WILLIAMS

"That's not all," continued Rice. "As Mrs. Breese's business adviser—I've
been handling all her affairs for months—I receive all cancelled checks from
her bank. This morning the National City called me up. I went down to see
them. The cashier showed me a check for ten thousand dollars made out to
this man and signed presumably by Mrs. Breese. It had come through the
mails, with a letter signed by this man, instructing the bank to deposit this
money to his account in Paris. Mr. Wilkins—the cashier—questioned the
signature. It seemed an obvious forgery to him. I agreed with him.

"I took the check and the letter and came here. Unfortunately Mrs. Breese
and this young man were out, so I left them in an envelope with a note for
Mrs. Breese, and put the envelope on this table. I had several engagements
and couldn't get in touch with Mrs. Breese until after dinner. Then I called
her up and asked her if she'd gotten my note. She hadn't. She knew nothing
about it. Then I asked her if she had made out a check for ten thousand dollars
to Thomas, and she knew nothing about that! Naturally she was upset and
angry. And an hour later I'm called at the American Ministry and told she's
been murdered. There are the facts!"

The actor had been striving vainly to interrupt him. Now he burst forth:
"It's a lie—I didn't forge any check. I don't know anything about it."

"Then where's the letter I left?" demanded Rice. "I left it right on this table.
You found it and tore it up, didn't you? Tore up all the evidence! Then, when
Mrs. Breese accused you of it, you lost your head and killed her. You didn't
think you'd be found out, did you?"

"But I don't know anything about a check! I never wrote a check!" The actor
turned to me pleadingly. Rice snorted impatiently. "There's a mistake," the
actor wailed weakly. "I never wrote that check. Why should I?"

"To get money so you could run off to Europe!"

"But I didn't need that money!"

"So you admit," Rice was triumphantly inquisitorial, "that you were running off to Europe with this girl in New York!"

"And what if I was?" demanded the actor. "There's nothing wrong in that. I was sick to death of this place. I didn't want to marry Mrs. Breese!"

"Just a minute," Smith intervened. "You say, Mr. Thomas, that you were making plans to go to Europe. Where did you expect to get the money for your trip?"

The actor paused, looked at Smith and then, truculently: "Mrs. Breese was giving it to me."

"That's news to me," snapped Rice. "And I'm her business adviser. I'd know if she was going to give you money."

"Just why," Smith demanded, "should Mrs. Breese give you that money? I think I ought to warn you, Mr. Thomas, that frankness may save you a lot of trouble at this time."

Thomas glared sullenly at Rice.

"I've got nothing to hide," he said. "I was getting tired of hanging around here where everybody looked on me as a poor relation. I told Mrs. Breese I wanted to get out. I said I needed some money, and she said she'd give it to me."

"A very generous woman," said Smith.

"Well, I stuck to her during the trial!" Thomas defended himself. "I had letters she wrote me that would have looked very bad. I played square with her and she appreciated it. She offered to settle twenty-five thousand dollars on me when I left here."

"When did she decide to do that?" demanded Smith.

"Tonight—after dinner. She was very nice about it, too. I told her about Miss Saunders, and she wished me luck! I guess I've got nothing to hide. You can't do anything to me. I've played square." His voice rose righteously.

Rice laughed. "That's a swell defence," he said. "You didn't forget the check. You were blackmailing her. Well, as a matter of fact, Mr. Wilkins at the National City Bank can testify to the check. He spotted it." He turned on Smith. "I've had enough of this nasty business. I can't stand here looking at him much longer. I'll be upstairs with the children if you should want me."

Rice left us, and we could hear his heavy footsteps stamping up the stairs.

After a pause, Smith said quietly: "Well, Mr. Thomas, what have you got to say for yourself?"

"Nothing!" rasped the actor. "Nothing!"

"Do you deny that you forged that check?" demanded Smith.

"I don't know anything about a check," Thomas shouted. "I've told you, haven't I?"

"Do you expect me to believe, Mr. Thomas, that Mrs. Breese voluntarily and cheerfully offered to pay you money so you could marry this Miss Saunders?"

"I don't care what you believe."

"Very well," said Smith quietly. "It's my duty to tell you, Mr. Thomas, that in all my experience I have never seen a clearer case of circumstantial evidence. You killed Mrs. Breese."

CHAPTER IX
THIRD DEGREE

"BUT I DIDN'T KILL anyone!" shouted the actor. "Good God, man, what do you want from me? I've had enough!" His voice screeched protest.

"Sit down," Smith ordered.

Reluctantly the actor obeyed, as if in a daze.

"I'll tell you the facts as we have them now. If you can offer anything to offset them, I'll be very glad to hear what you have to say. But this is the way the thing would appear in court:

"You are a member of Mrs. Breese's household. Your status is peculiar. The talk is that you're her fiancé. But you have a sweetheart in New York who expects to go to Europe with you. You have no money. Mr. Rice and the National City Bank testify that they have seen a forged check made out by you. Mr. Rice testifies that he telephoned Mrs. Breese tonight informing her of the check. Mrs. Breese taxes you with it."

"But she didn't," protested the actor. "I went upstairs while she was still telephoning."

"Why?"

"To write a letter to Miss Saunders. Mrs. Breese had agreed to give me the money and I was sending a letter to Miss Saunders to tell her everything was all set. Then, when I was about to come down again, the butler ran up to tell me she had been killed!"

"You still deny you forged this check Mr. Rice mentioned?"

"Absolutely!"

"All right," said Smith. "Let's waive that. In any case, fifteen minutes after Rice phoned here, Mrs. Breese is found dead. You're upstairs. The butler tells you that Mrs. Breese has been killed. You don't send for a doctor. Why? Because you knew already that Mrs. Breese was dead. You send him for a policeman."

"I didn't think."

"Perhaps not. In any case, Mr. Thomas, you had the opportunity to kill Mrs. Breese, and if I am to believe Rice, you had the motive. I'm being very frank with you."

"But I didn't do it! I didn't do it!"

Smith shrugged his shoulders.

"Have you ever fired a revolver, Mr. Thomas?" he demanded.

"Have I ever—yes, in the army."

"Are you a pretty good shot?"

"Not especially so, no. But I've never fired a revolver since. I never even had one in my hand."

I stared at Thomas, for at that moment I recalled one of the hectic events of the yacht trip down.

"Don't you remember," I said, "that on the yacht you went into Henry Breese's cabin late at night and took a revolver from his luggage?"

"Oh!" the actor looked daggers at me. I, too, apparently had turned against him. "That was after he tried to throw himself in the ocean, and I knew he had a revolver, and I wasn't taking any chances. So I took it away from him."

"What happened to that revolver?" Smith demanded.

"I threw it away that night."

"Sorry to contradict you," I said firmly. "You threw the cartridges away. I distinctly remember seeing you put that revolver in your pocket."

"I threw it away later!"

Smith surveyed the actor through half-lidded eyes.

"Any particular reason for the delay?" he inquired.

The actor shrugged his shoulders. "No. I just didn't know what to do about it. It was dashed unpleasant for me. Everybody on the boat saying that boy wanted to kill himself on account of me. I knew it was a fake. But I wasn't sure. It was dashed unpleasant!" He whipped out a lavender silk handkerchief and delicately patted his brow. "I've had nothing but bad luck since we left New York. I wish to God I'd never gone on this trip."

"Ye-es," drawled Smith. "You've had a lot of bad breaks." He looked up at the ceiling. "By the way, you don't happen to know if Mrs. Breese left a will?"

"How should I know?" The actor carefully avoided my glance. "I wasn't in Mrs. Breese's confidence to that extent. I was just a friend."

"But you were engaged to her, weren't you?" Smith asked.

"Well, in a way. I didn't have anything to do with it."

"Are you in the habit of permitting women to engage themselves to you?" demanded Smith.

"Oh——" The actor squirmed. "You don't understand. Dora was full of whims. She didn't mean anything by it. She wasn't seriously engaged."

"I see," said Smith. "It was just a joke."

"Well, dash it all," cried the actor, "what could I do? I couldn't very well tell her I was engaged already. I was her guest. I didn't want to offend her."

Smith smiled drily. "Yeah, that'd be bad manners. Now, Mr. Thomas, I'm not up on social etiquette, but here's something that needs explaining. On the boat coming down Mrs. Breese announced her engagement to you; when did she break it?"

"Why—she never broke it exactly. After all that fuss on the boat, why, Dora said we'd have to wait. I was glad of it! Then today I told her about my girl. She wished me luck. And everything was fine!"

"I'm trying my best to understand," said Smith. "You and Mrs. Breese were engaged, but when you told her you had a previous engagement, she just said: 'Great!' Is that it?"

"Well, Dora wouldn't stand in the way of my happiness."

"So much so," continued Smith, "that she was going to give you a very substantial wedding present. A lot of money." He paused significantly. "What for?"

"What for?" the actor repeated. "She knew I didn't have any money, and I stuck to her, didn't I? I went through hell for her in the trial, didn't I? Dash it all, she had some gratitude left. You don't seem to understand. Dora and I have been friends for years. I've spent a lot of my time in Dora's interests—taking her out, looking after things, seeing that she was comfortable. Dash it all, a woman appreciates that."

"And she wasn't sore about this other girl?" demanded Smith. "Not the least bit jealous?"

The actor smiled. "Oh, well, you can't help that." He swaggered a bit. "You couldn't very well expect anything else, could you?"

"Well, in my own roughneck way," said Smith, "I'd expect her to blow up and throw you out of the house."

"She couldn't do that!" said the actor. "She wrote me a lot of letters she wouldn't want in the wrong hands. Not that I'd do anything like that! That's blackmail. That's despicable! Dora was too nice—had too much pride—to make a fuss about things.... You mustn't believe that man Rice," he pleaded. "Dora and I never quarrelled for a minute. We were real friends. This is a terrible blow to me!"

"Yes," said Smith, "I see that."

The actor glared at him. "Is that meant for sarcasm?"

Smith nodded obligingly.

"Then it's in very poor taste."

"That may be," said Smith, "but of all the thin alibis I've ever heard, yours takes the prize."

"Alibis?" shouted the actor. "I didn't kill her! I don't need an alibi."

"I'm not saying you killed her," said Smith.

"Well, you're intimating!" the actor bit his lips in his anger. "What are you asking all those questions for? I've told you all I know. I guess I've got some rights. And I've got some friends, too." He was incoherent in his sudden fury. "You'd better be careful how you treat me."

He moved to the door.

"I'm going!" he shouted.

"I'm not stopping you," said Smith. "But you'd better not go too far." He smiled grimly. "I mean that both ways. I don't want you to leave the house, Mr. Thomas. I'm not through with you yet—not by a long shot!"

"I'm leaving for New York right now!" the actor shrieked defiantly.

"Come here!" growled Smith.

The actor glared at him hesitantly. Smith advanced on him. "I don't like your attitude," said Smith. "I wasn't ready to arrest you—yet. But you're forcing my hand. Also you're being very dumb about it."

"Am I?" the actor cried. "I'll have no more of your insults! I won't stand it, I tell you!"

Smith laughed suddenly. I turned in surprise at him.

"That's all I wanted to know," he said, still chuckling. "I wanted to see if you could get good and mad, Mr. Thomas. You can!"

The actor was breathing heavily. "Let me go!" he cried. "What are you doing to me? I don't know anything about it. I'm going back to New York."

Smith suddenly reached for the actor's arm and held it securely. Thomas cried out in pain.

"You're not going to New York," said Smith. "You're going to stay right here with me. If you didn't kill Mrs. Breese, you know who did."

"I don't!" the actor protested. "Let me go, won't you? Let me go!"

I was so intent in watching this third-degree that for a moment I did not hear the sounds of scuffling and angry voices in the reception-room. Before we were quite aware of it, a young man was being dragged before us by the butler, now very red-faced, and the Japanese steward. Both captors were out of breath and talking at once. Only their prisoner seemed calm and perfectly self-possessed.

"Caught him—hiding—in the blue room—just now," the butler panted.

Then as they propelled their captive toward us, where the full light of the chandelier enveloped him, I could not but gasp. For the young man so unceremoniously brought before us was Perutkin's melancholy protégé, the Count Giering-Trelovitch.

Thomas seemed to recognize him, too, for the actor's expression changed as if magically. His fear left him and I saw him grin in relief.

"There's the man you want!" he cried.

CHAPTER X
THE COUNT CONFESSES

THE COUNT BOWED AND said quietly: "Yes, gentlemen, I guess I am the man you want."

He turned to Smith.

"You are of the police?"

"Yes," said Smith.

"What is it you wish to know?" asked the Count gently.

"What does he wish to know?" the actor intervened scornfully. "I'll tell you. This man was Mrs. Breese's son-in-law. He murdered a man in Riga. He's hated Mrs. Breese ever since she made the Countess divorce him. He's been following her all over the world. She's complained to me about him a dozen times." He paused for breath. "And then you have the audacity to annoy *me*! Dash it all, I've got a good mind to sue you for damages!" He looked accusingly at the Count. "Come ahead, tell them you did it and be done with it. I'm going back to New York tonight! I can't waste any more time in this dashed hole."

The Count smiled sadly. "I'm sorry to have inconvenienced you, Mr. Thomas," he said. "I had no idea I was a source of annoyance to you. Now, if you will leave me alone with this officer, I think we can straighten matters out very quickly."

"I'm going!" cried Thomas. "I'm going. And this time nobody's going to stop me!"

"You stay upstairs," said Smith, "until I tell you to go!"

He turned to the Russian, barking: "Well, where do you come in?"

"I'm afraid," the Russian smiled, "I came in at the wrong time. I have something to tell you, officer."

"Yes? What is it?"

"First, I want you to send for Miss Breese, my former wife."

"First tell me how you got here," countered Smith.

"I'm afraid I can't agree," the Count shook his head. "Will you be good enough to send for Miss Breese?"

"Maybe. First, I want to ask you something."

"Yes?" The man seemed perfectly at ease, strangely enough.

"What were you hiding upstairs for?"

"I'm not ready to tell you that—yet."

Smith surveyed him coldly. "You know that Mrs. Breese was murdered tonight?" He pointed to the body.

"Yes, I know."

"Who told you?"

"No one. I have eyes." The Count indicated the body pityingly.

"Do you know who killed Mrs. Breese?"

"Yes," said the Russian. "I do."

His voice trembled slightly.

"What's that?" cried Smith, startled.

"I said: 'Yes, I do know.'"

"Who was it?" snapped Smith.

"I shall be glad to tell you," replied the Russian calmly, "after I've seen the Countess. But certainly not before. Will you be good enough to send for her? I ask you again."

Smith studied this strange phenomenon before he replied. He looked at me out of the corner of his eye to indicate his bewilderment.

"Please understand," the Count continued, "whatever I have to say I shall say to Miss Breese. To no one else."

"All right," said Smith, gesturing to the butler. "Get Miss Breese down here." The butler hurried off. The Count looked about him. He stared at the body.

"I don't want Miss Breese to come into this room. It would not be advisable," he said. "And in any case, I wish to talk to her alone. I want you two gentlemen to wait here, at this door. You will hold it slightly open, so that you may listen to what I have to say. I don't want Miss Breese to know we're being watched. I want her to feel that we are quite alone, especially as it may be the last time." He paused, and smiled bitterly. Then he waved a white hand apologetically. "You perhaps do not understand me. C'est bien. The only thing to remember for you gentlemen is: you will stay, please, right here."

"You're much too insistent about that," said Smith suspiciously. "Wait a minute! You were caught hiding in this house. How do I know you aren't trying to get away—shoving us behind this door?"

"How can I get away?" demanded the Count quietly. "You will be right here. You can have a revolver pointed at me, if you wish." His gentleness left him and he was sharp and incisive. He was now giving commands. "Understand—you will either follow my suggestion or I shall say nothing."

Before Smith could reply, we heard footsteps, and the Count opened the door. He strode out into the reception-room, carefully closing the door behind him so that we were left barely a crack through which to peep. Smith just as carefully widened the crack, and we caught a glimpse of Mary Breese descending the stairs. She was deathly pale, and her eyes were lost in mourning shadows.

There was not enough room for the two of us, so Smith monopolized the sight. I strained to listen to the scene I could not see. But I noticed that Smith was following the Russian's suggestions to the letter. His right hand was at his revolver holster.

I heard the Count cry: "Mary!"

A pause.

Then I heard her move toward him, crying incoherently: "Isn't it awful! I need you so!"

I heard him trying to comfort her gently. She was sobbing unrestrainedly now.

"Please, Mary ... please ... you mustn't." The Count's voice broke now.

I heard her say: "It would never have happened if I hadn't let you go—I needed you so! But what could I do?"

"No," he said slowly, "it would never have happened."

"You mustn't leave me now!" she cried. "You mustn't ever leave me!"

Silence. Then, as if the words were wrung from him: "Why didn't you—why didn't you try to see me as I begged you? You got my letters, didn't you?"

"No, I didn't get any letters. What letters? I didn't even know you were in town! I don't know that you're here now! I—oh, I don't know anything any more!"

"Please—don't cry. Didn't I tell you I phoned. I wrote. I tried every way to see you."

"No!" Then as if in agonized appeal: "Don't leave me—please don't leave me!"

It was not difficult to patch together from their incoherent appeals to each other the story of the strange relationship. Someone in the household—Mrs. Breese, undoubtedly—had been determined that the Russian be kept from his former wife. I remembered how he had told me, the night Perutkin had brought me to him, that he had exhausted every possible means of communicating with Mary Breese. It was clear to me now that Mary Breese had not willingly parted from her husband.

But my reflections were disturbed suddenly. I had paid but desultory attention to their mutual efforts to comfort each other. Then I heard the Russian say:

"Mary, I don't know how to tell you this—you've had enough to bear—but I must tell you. I must! Listen to me!"

Silence.

Smith leaned forward.

"I came here tonight to see you. I knew that if I could talk to you, hold you—but I mustn't talk about that. I got in through the garden window, in the back. I dodged all the servants until I got in here. Mary, your mother saw me!"

Silence again. Then the girl's dazed voice: "Mother—saw you?"

"Yes—she—Mary, I must have been crazy. Mary, I don't know what happened. I must have been crazy! Mary, I—I killed her!"

I heard the girl's piercing scream!

Then, as Smith leaped forward, the door slammed in our faces. A key turned. The lock clicked. Smith hammered on the door, hurling himself at it.

We heard voices, running feet.

The next moment a stupefied servant opened the door. Smith and I ran out. We saw the girl crumpled in a heap on the stairs. She had fainted. Hurriedly, Smith gave orders to carry her upstairs.

We ran out upon the terrace. We heard nothing but the soft rustling of leaves. We hurried down into the street.

But the Count had disappeared.

CHAPTER XI
THE PSYCHOLOGICAL ALIBI

IT WAS THE NEXT morning that Boris Sergeivitch Perutkin actively intervened in the Murder in the Gilded Cage, as I called it. Smith sent for him. I still remember how the giant stamped into Smith's cubby-hole of an office, his big face radiating geniality, his little eyes twinkling with malicious humor.

"At last!" he greeted Smith. "At last, you have the common sense to summon me!"

"I didn't call you in as a detective," said Smith, "I've sent for you as a friend of this Count."

"So!" the Russian grinned. "I am disappointed."

"Where is he?" barked Smith.

"My good friend," replied the detective, "I haven't any idea where he is."

He seated himself in the hard wicker chair Smith kept for guests, lit a cigar, and puffed lazily.

"I saw him for perhaps five minutes after he left you last night, and since then he has been swallowed by the world."

Smith went to the window and opened it. A refreshing morning breeze floated in, bearing upon its wings the cries of the Chinese street vendors below.

"Listen, Perutkin," said Smith. "I'm in no mood for jokes. I'm going to get at the bottom of this and damn soon, too. I want to know what's the idea. I had a perfect case against this actor before your friend breezed in. He comes through with a confession and he beats it. Why?"

"Well," said the Russian, "my friend is not a practical joker. He wouldn't perpetrate anything in such bad taste. He must have his reasons."

"It was a cheap trick!" Smith fumed. "Telling us to watch behind the door. 'If you don't trust me, have a revolver in your hand.' And then taking the key with him, and locking us in!"

Smith walked about angrily.

The Russian laughed. "He followed my orders to the letter."

Smith stopped and stared at him. "You mean to say you told him to do that?"

"Certainly, my friend," said Perutkin. "I am his advisor. He asked me what to do. I told him."

"Oh! He asked you what to do!" mocked Smith. "Then you'll kindly come across right now and tell me what it's all about."

"Unfortunately," said the Russian, "I don't know myself. The Count went to the house without my knowledge. He telephoned me from the house, and if you want me to repeat the conversation, I shall be glad to. He said: 'Boris Sergeivitch, I want to confess a murder.' Just like that. And I said: 'My friend, are you mad?' And he said: 'I want to confess a murder. The police are downstairs. But I don't wish to pay the penalty.' Well, I am his friend. I cannot ask him on the telephone: 'What? Where?' I gave him my advice. He acted accordingly. And that," the Russian concluded, "is all I know."

"You haven't seen him since?" Smith asked.

Perutkin shook his head.

"Well, you know where you can get him, don't you?"

"I might," conceded the Russian. His little eyes gleamed suddenly. "I have a bargain to make with you. I have the best possible reasons in the world for being interested in this case. It fits in so completely with a case that absorbed me not so long ago, that is still not solved. Besides, I am aching for work, as I have told you. I shall find my friend, the Count, for you, and you can do with him what you wish. But on one condition."

"What's that?"

"That you give me a free hand in the investigation." As Smith began to protest, he added: "Understand, I want no credit. I want no official status. I seek no kudos. I have a definite purpose in mind. If you help me, I shall help you." Then, pleading, "Believe me, you shall not regret your decision. Then it is agreed!" Before Smith could even answer!

"Wait a minute," Smith interrupted. "Just exactly what do you want?"

"Access to Mrs. Breese's house, and all the facts as they are disclosed. Nothing more."

Smith nodded. "That's all right," he said. "I don't see any harm in that. But you must produce the Count within one week or I shall have you arrested as accessory to the crime."

"Done!" exclaimed the Russian. "Now, Mr. Smith, you may rest easy. I shall untangle this little problem for you. First, the facts!"

"Facts!" growled Smith. "I wish I knew what they were!"

He outlined what he had gathered thus far, beginning with our interview with the elder Breese where we had first learned of the murder. Boris Sergeivitch Perutkin listened intently, grunting at each significant piece of evidence, gesturing impatiently at routine detail.

"The big things I want to know," he would interrupt. "Never mind the measurements of the floor. I am not a scientific detective. I live in reality. Proceed, please."

"Here's the thing in a nutshell," concluded Smith. "Until your friend butted in, I had a reasonably clear case against the actor. He's a bad egg. He had a girl back in New York. He needed money. There's that forged check. There's Rice's testimony. It all fits in. And yet along comes your friend with a confession and—there we are! Now what do you make of it?"

"At present, nothing," said the Russian. "First, I must see the house. Will you accompany me?"

"Oh, I've been all over the place," said Smith. "There's nothing there."

"Perhaps not," replied the Russian. "But I must insist upon seeing that room. It is all-important."

Smith turned to me. "All right, why don't you go with him? I've got a report to fill out now. I'll telephone ahead for them to let you in. I may meet you there later."

"Good," exclaimed the Russian, smiling at me. "I like an audience when I work. So will you come, please?"

Smith stopped us at the door.

"By the way," he said to the Russian, "I've got the medical examiner's report here, if you care to see it. I've just had it translated into English!"

He handed a sheaf of papers to the Russian, who scanned them hastily and thrust them into his pocket.

"I shall examine them later. Probably they contain nothing more than you've already told me."

"Not much more," said Smith, turning back to his work. "And if you see anything in the house I've overlooked, I'll eat it. If you take my advice, never mind the house, and get hold of your friend, the Count. That's more important."

"We shall see," said the Russian. And to me: "Come, my friend."

Down in the street we were fortunate enough to find a brand-new taxi and with incredible speed we raced through the choked streets of the business quarter, narrowly dodging other cars and at least four trams. We stopped at a kiosk for the morning papers. The Gilded Cage was the story of the day. Although there were but scanty available facts, these were embellished with considerable gossip, and smeared over the front pages of both Cuban and English papers.

Apparently the murder had aroused considerable interest at home, too, for cables from New York recounted the shock of Mrs. Breese's friends at the news. Considerable space was given to a rehash of the divorce trial.

When we drew up before the Gilded Cage, we found an assorted crowd of curiosity seekers lined up in front of us. Several of the native newspaper men were sipping bacardi and coca-cola in the corner café across the street. A lone and perspiring photographer was taking pictures from all angles of the house of mystery. A murder sensation was well under way.

Smith had notified the native police on guard of our coming, so we were admitted without much delay. I led the Russian at his request into the drawing-room and roughly mapped out for him the position of the body as I had last seen it. We were alone.

One of the policemen told us that the family was upstairs, and we left orders that we were not to be disturbed in our examination. As I read off my copious notes of the day before, the Russian seemed only casually interested. When I was done, he said: "It is a fallacy to take so many notes. One does not see the forest for the trees, as you say in your country. But thank you!"

Then he brushed me aside and began examining the furniture:

"Fine pieces!" he commented. "I have a love for expensive old furniture. But what is this doing here?" He pointed to the black and silver radio. "It is out of harmony. I do not like it."

I could not very well point out to him that we were not there to criticize the color scheme of the drawing-room. He walked about, smoking his big cigar, examining the pictures and then pausing at the bust of Mrs. Breese.

"What a woman!" he exclaimed, patting the stone head. "Unhappy woman! Always restless, always scheming, never satisfied." He shook his head mournfully and then: "She had very poor taste! Very poor! In furniture, in people." Then he wheeled at me suddenly. "Behold! You think I am wasting time? I am! I am getting my thoughts together. I see something. What is more important, I feel something. I shall talk to you—I shall think aloud, as we say. Behold the problem that confronts me. A woman is murdered."

"There were fifteen servants and three members of the household, the actor and two children. We take the actor first. The evidence is overwhelming against him. He is a bad character. He has another woman. He needs money. He has forged a check. He has been found out. It is perfect! Too perfect! No man would commit murder under such circumstances, at least if he were sane, and Mr. Thomas is stupid but sane.

"Mr. Rice is the one who accuses Mr. Thomas. Now, where was Mr. Rice last evening? That is important to know."

"Why, you don't for a moment think," I said, "that Rice did it? He was Mrs. Breese's friend. Her adviser."

"When a man accuses another of a murder, his hands must be clean. Spotless. Where was Mr. Rice last night? That is what I ask."

"As a matter of fact, I just remember now that Smith checked up on Rice this morning," I said. "It was so much a matter of routine that I paid no particular attention to it. Rice dined at the American Ministry last night. As I remember it, he got there at nine and never left the presence of the Minister except for five minutes once to telephone. It would take anyone an hour to go from this house to the Ministry. So that leaves Rice out definitely."

"Yes," agreed the Russian, "that leaves Mr. Rice out. And yet Mr. Rice is very anxious to accuse Mr. Thomas. Why?"

"Because he doesn't like him," I suggested. "Because he sincerely believes Thomas did it."

"Not good enough," said the Russian. "But let us proceed. For I have a point to make. The methodical Mr. Smith collects an excellent case against Mr. Thomas. Until my friend, the Count, suddenly appears and confesses.

"Let us consider my friend, the Count. What was he doing in the house? That is no secret. To you, I can talk. You have sentiment in your soul. Your Mr. Smith has none. He has been trying to see his former wife, Mary Breese. He loves her. They have been separated by the calamitous event in Riga, plus Mrs. Breese's interference. You can build up an excellent case against my friend, the Count. In the first place, he has already been suspected of one murder. Then, he has no love for Mrs. Breese. He has been cast out. Presumably, he took his revenge. And yet I know the man. That is not him!

"But he confesses and escapes. Why? He didn't tell me, and yet I know. While he was in this house, waiting to see Mary Breese, he stumbled upon something which led him to make his confession. Remember—he loves this girl deeply. He knows that she is suffering—a terrible shock. Suppose that he learns something that will hurt her even more terribly?"

"I don't follow," I protested.

"Let me make myself plain. Mary Breese is horrified at the murder of her mother. Naturally. It is sufficient tragedy for anyone. But if someone very close and dear to Mary Breese were the murderer the shock would be double, would it not? It would be an enormous tragedy. She might not survive it. In any case, the Count would try to shield her from the knowledge. He is chivalrous enough, foolish enough, if you will. Now—" the Russian fixed his little eyes on me—"whom is he trying to shield? Someone very dear to Mary Breese. Her brother?"

"It hardly seems possible," I said.

"Granted that—for the moment. There is her father."

"Old Man Breese? Not much!" I scoffed.

"But why not?" he demanded.

"For one thing," I said "because he was in the hotel with us when we got the news."

The Russian smiled and shook his head admiringly. "It would be diabolically clever—so ingenuous. Don't you see?" I caught a curious excitement in his voice. "Behold the psychological alibi! Don't you see it?"

"I'm afraid I don't," I shook my head.

"Ach!" the Russian snorted impatiently. "Behold! Let us say that Mr. Breese wanted to kill his wife. Now, the unfortunate lady was killed at about nine-fifteen. What time was your engagement with Mr. Breese?"

"At ten!"

"Excellent! He calls Smith up in the morning and makes an engagement with him for ten o'clock that night. Do you see? He comes here at nine-fifteen, kills his wife, takes a taxi and gets back to the hotel at least ten minutes before you arrive. He tells you that he fears something is going to happen to Mrs. Breese. He plants very obviously suspicion against the actor. While you are there, he receives a phone call informing him of his wife's murder. Psychologically, he impresses you with his alibi. You do not reason that he may have gone out and just returned. Because you are there with him when he receives the news, you believe he is just as innocent and ignorant of the crime as you are. But it is diabolically clever!"

CHAPTER XII
THE SUSPECT REFUSES TO TALK

THE PSYCHOLOGICAL ALIBI! As the Russian's theory dawned on me I was shocked to find that every detail clicked into place. Breese *had* summoned us to his hotel exactly three-quarters of an hour after the murder had been committed. His entire demeanor during the interview now seemed highly suspicious to me.

I rose from my chair determinedly and reached for the telephone.

"I'm going to call up Ben Smith," I said, "and tell him about this."

But the Russian stopped me.

"You'll do nothing of the kind," he said. "You are entirely too hasty, my friend. I have given you a theory, and you have jumped to a conclusion."

I resented the Russian's assumption of superiority. I resented his amusement at my haste. Possibly it was because of this that I sought to destroy his reasoned conclusions. I remember I said: "Perhaps I am hasty. After all there's no motive."

The Russian smiled.

"But what motive would he have?" I protested.

"Motive? His wife has dragged his name into scandal. Despite her foolishness she emerged triumphant from the divorce trial. He was hopelessly beaten. His own children turned against him. He comes down here, swallowing his pride and begging for a reconciliation. His wife will not see him. His children will not see him. He admits as much, doesn't he? He learns his wife wants to marry this actor. Mr. Breese is an old man. His pride is gone. His home is gone. His children are gone.

"Consider his character. He is not used to defeat. He is a man who has had his own way. He is a hard man, obstinate. And who is to blame for his position? Put yourself in his place. Can't you see a steadily growing malignant hatred of his wife? I assure you, men have committed murder for much less!

"And see how it all fits in," the Russian continued. "Why does Rice accuse the actor? Because Mr. Breese has talked to him. He has given Rice the telegrams from the detective agency. He has poisoned Rice's mind with suspicion, just as he planned to poison Smith's mind when he summoned him for an engagement three-quarters of an hour after the murder.

"And see how the confession of my friend, the Count, fits into this! Suppose he had seen Mr. Breese murder his wife. Wouldn't it be like my friend to try and save Mary Breese from the double tragedy? Her mother dead, her father a murderer? Now put yourself in the Count's place. Knowing what he knows, what is he to do? Loving Mary Breese as he loves her, what is he to do?

"It would be a problem for any man. My friend, the Count, hides in one of the rooms upstairs. He telephones me, and asks for advice. I tell him. He lets himself be discovered. He is dragged before Smith. He knows the real murderer. At first his impulse was to take the blame upon himself together with the consequences. But my friend is no story-book hero. He has no desire to spend the rest of his life in a Cuban prison. So, following my suggestion, he arranges for you to overhear his confession, and then he disappears. Mr. Breese is protected. Mary Breese is saved from a horrible truth. Now, my friend, is it not probable? Is it not reasonable?"

"Well," I hesitated, "it sounds reasonable enough. But there's one thing you forget."

"And that is?"

"No one knows Mr. Breese was here. No one saw him here. The servants testify there were no visitors. How did Mr. Breese get in?"

"That," said the Russian, "is not as difficult as it sounds. How did my friend, the Count, get in? But I'll concede you have touched, without knowing it, a very vital problem here, something I hope to solve before the day is over. At least, if Mr. Breese does what I think he will."

He strode over to the garden window, and drew the curtains aside, so that a bright sun streamed through the room. He looked out upon the brilliant foliage of the garden.

"To think," he mused, "that a house built for beauty and grandeur should house meanness and murder! But that is the way of human beings. It was like this several years ago—when the Baron was murdered. Outwardly all peace and contentment and inwardly a ghastly tragedy." He turned from the window. "Do you remember, I said, when I heard that Mr. Breese had arrived in this city: 'The circle is complete'? My friend, I am firmly convinced that the man who killed the Baron is responsible for the death of Mrs. Breese!"

"But where? How? I fail to see the connection!"

"It is there, nevertheless. I don't know. I feel it. The same people were there in Riga—Mr. Breese, Mr. Rice, Mr. Thomas, my friend the Count, the Countess, the boy—they were all there. Isn't it curious to you? Isn't it significant?"

He paused abruptly.

"I was right!" He pointed to the street, and I moved to the window to see. "Mr. Breese is about to pay us a visit. Here, quick, get hold of the policemen in the reception-room and tell them on no account to open the door!"

"But why?"

"Don't question. Do as I say."

Wonderingly, I obeyed. Before I could return to the drawing-room, a bell pealed. The policeman made no move. Again the bell, and again. The Russian strode out into the hall. I followed.

Five minutes passed, the bell resounded now through the house. Still we made no move.

Finally I heard the click of a key in the lock. The door opened. Mr. Breese looked up at us.

"That," said the Russian, his little eyes gleaming, "is how Mr. Breese came in."

"Who is this man?" Breese demanded of me.

Before I could reply, the Russian continued: "Absurdly simple, isn't it? I forgot, Mr. Breese, that you built this house. Naturally you would have a key!"

"What in the world are you talking about?" Breese snapped. "Who is this man?"

I explained the Russian away as an associate of Smith's.

"Surely, you must remember me," said the Russian. "Don't you remember in Riga—I was then with the Russian police. We had an interesting talk then. We'll have another interesting talk now. Won't you step in here, Mr. Breese?"

"I don't know you and I don't remember you," Breese barked. "I've come here to see my children. I haven't come to see you. If you're a detective, let me see your credentials."

"I haven't any," the Russian replied, "but Mr. Smith will vouch for me."

"I don't care who vouches for you. You might have some consideration for a man in my position. Please get out of my way. I'm going upstairs."

"Very well, sir," the Russian bowed. Without a word, Breese laboriously began climbing the wide stone steps.

When he was out of sight, the Russian grinned good-naturedly: "The suspect refuses to talk!"

CHAPTER XIII

MR. BREESE IS ANXIOUS

WHEN Ben Smith arrived an hour later he found us smoking placidly in the drawing-room. The Russian was at ease in one of the huge chairs, his big head bowed to his barrel chest, his sharp little eyes now half closed. The afternoon sun was blazing hot, and even the heavy brocaded curtains could not smother its discomfort. There had been a half-somnolent silence between us for some time now.

"Working hard?" Smith greeted us grinning, very cool and dapper in his immaculate linen suit. Smith was obviously amused at the slothful ease of the Russian at the scene of the crime.

"Eh?" The Russian lifted his head and blinked. I could see now that if it were not for Smith's interruption he would have fallen asleep. He smiled confidingly. "I was just preparing myself for a little siesta." He shook his head vigorously as if to wake himself. "It is so confoundedly hot in this country," he sighed. "And, besides, I think my work is done."

"What's that?" inquired Smith sharply. I looked up, too, for the Russian had given me no evidence that he had stumbled upon any vital factor in the tangled case.

"Certainly," said the Russian. "My work is done. I have just been expounding to our friend here my theory of the case. I shall tell it to you. It concerns Mr. Breese."

I sat back once more while the Russian repeated his speculations on the status and activities of the elder Breese, but Smith was evidently unimpressed and sought to interrupt the tale several times. He felt and said that the Russian jumped at conclusions entirely too glibly.

"I don't know how you do things in Russia, but we work differently where I come from," Smith pointed out. "Your main case against old man Breese rests on the fact that he *might* have come here, that he *might* have hated his wife sufficiently to kill her, that he *might* have planned an alibi by calling me to his hotel after the murder. You can't prove any of these three points.

"On the other hand, I've got a definite confession from the Count and a clear circumstantial case against the actor. It's all very well in detective stories to reach way out for your suspect, but take it from me, in my experience the man who looks guilty generally is. I can answer every point you make against Breese."

"Do so!" challenged the Russian. "You concede that Mr. Breese had the key to this house and might have entered unseen?"

"Certainly," said Smith. "But let's call up the hotel and find out if he left his rooms last night. That's more to the point, isn't it? Merely possessing the key means nothing."

"He could have left his hotel unseen," said the Russian. "Or he could bribe any employee likely to see him."

"Then there's no use even checking up on him?" demanded Smith sarcastically.

"None at all," replied the Russian easily. "You do not deny that Mr. Breese had a motive?"

"Certainly I deny it," retorted Smith. "What did he have to gain by the murder?"

"His children!" the Russian answered.

"Ah!" said Smith. "Do you think a man would deliberately kill his wife to get custody of his children?"

"But why not?" demanded the Russian. "It is natural."

"It's ridiculous," said Smith. "I don't go with you there at all. And now take your friend, the Count—why do you assume he confessed to save anybody? He had plenty of motive to kill Mrs. Breese. He certainly had the opportunity. Why do you assume the confession isn't genuine?"

"But he would not kill," protested the Russian. "I know his character."

"And I give you the same answer on old man Breese," retorted Smith. "I've watched him pretty carefully. He's not the type either."

"So? You know why you say that? Because he is a wealthy man and respectable."

"What's that got to do with it?" demanded Smith.

"Everything," replied the Russian. "You Americans have a religious awe of wealth and respectability. But don't you know, my friend, that in a case such as this, where robbery is not a motive, it is precisely the wealthy and respectable whom we must study for our suspect? If Mr. Breese were a day laborer, you would readily admit he killed his wife, with whom he had frequent disagreements, in a moment of passionate rage. But you will not concede that basically Mr. Breese is as the day laborer—just as violent, just as primitive. I suppose you will call this point of view Russian. Believe me, my friend, it is universal. I speak from experience."

The Russian rose to his full height, and with the pedantic air of a lecturer continued:

"I cite you one of the most brutal murders in Petrograd. A ballet dancer is found in the Neva, her body hacked to pieces. The work of a thug, an apache, you say? No! I found a worthy lawyer, a model citizen, an affectionate father, a devoted son, and in two days I had his confession. This dancer had threatened to tell his wife of their affair, and in his anger he had killed her."

"What's that got to do with old man Breese?" Smith demanded impatiently.

"Only this," replied the Russian. "Mr. Breese's wealth and respectability do not preclude him from being a murderer."

"All right, you win," Smith grinned wrily. "Only I'm not paid to be a debater. I'm paid to get the man who killed Mrs. Breese."

"And I've gotten him for you," said the Russian. "He's upstairs. Why not call him down and confront him? I tried to question him myself but without success."

"I'd just as soon send for Machado, the president of this country," Smith growled. "Think I'm crazy? What would I have to say to the old man? 'I understand you *might* have killed your wife.' Do you want me to say that?"

"No," said the Russian. "I shall tell you what to ask him. Behold! Mrs. Breese's will is to be read today and the funeral held shortly. If Mr. Breese is, as I am convinced, the man you want, he will be very anxious to clear out as quickly as possible. Isn't that natural?"

Smith nodded.

"Suppose you call him down and say to him: 'Mr. Breese, it is not necessary for you to remain for further investigation. The Count has confessed, and we have just arrested him. The case is over.'"

"What then?" demanded Smith.

"If," continued the Russian, "Mr. Breese confides to you that he will stay to take charge of the funeral arrangements and look after the children—that he is in no hurry to leave—we may assume that he is not overly anxious to get away from the scene of the crime and the possible danger of arrest. But, on the other hand—let us say, he is guilty. Then, knowing the Count is innocent, that inquiry may show his innocence, Mr. Breese will try to get away from here just as quickly as he can. Therefore, I say to you: Tell him the Count is arrested. He can leave immediately. And then see his reaction."

"Well," said Smith, grudgingly, "I don't see much point to it but I'm always perfectly willing to try anything. Where is he?"

But it was unnecessary for the Russian to reply. Mr. Breese himself opened the door and with an apologetic cough addressed the Russian: "I'm afraid I was rather rude to you a little while ago. I didn't mean to be."

"That's quite all right," murmured the Russian. "I was telling Mr. Smith just now that you are much distressed by the tragic events and it is quite understandable that your nerves are not what they should be."

Mr. Breese nodded. "I can't believe it's true yet," he murmured stonily. Then with an obvious effort at casualness: "You mentioned something about a key as I came in here. I suppose you questioned the fact that I possess a key and the house really belongs to my wife. Well, the fact is that I found this key in my trunk with some others this morning. I remember my agent gave me several at the time I first opened this house. And I brought it around in case it was needed."

Even to Smith this roundabout explanation must have seemed lame, for I saw him watching the old man with new interest.

And then Smith said: "By the way, Mr. Breese, there have been some developments I think you ought to know."

Breese turned to him quickly. His granite eyes lit up. I'm not sure, but it seemed to me that his right hand, resting upon a malacca stick, trembled slightly.

"We've made an arrest," Smith continued smoothly. For a moment Mr. Breese said nothing. Finally he found his voice. "Who is it?" he demanded.

"Well, I can't even pronounce his name," Smith confessed. "It's this Count Giering-Trelovitch—I think that's the name. Your former son-in-law."

"Impossible!" exclaimed the old man. "He had nothing to do with it." He stammered in his sudden excitement. "Look here—you've got the wrong man. Why, I understood you were proceeding against the actor. At least so Rice told me. Did he tell you about the forged check? And those telegrams?"

"I know," said Smith, "but the Count has made a confession."

The old man stared at Smith in amazement. "A confession?" he repeated blankly.

"Yes," said Smith. "Hasn't your daughter told you? He made the confession to her yesterday and disappeared. We got him a little while ago."

The old man shook his head. He said nothing.

"At first," continued Smith, "we thought the Count was acting out of pure chivalry. Trying to protect someone else. But we've finally swung around and we're taking the confession at face value." As the old man remained silent, Smith concluded. "So, Mr. Breese, I don't think we'll need you further. Unless the Count recants, we've got clear sailing."

"Yes, yes," murmured the old man, as if he did not hear what Smith was saying. The Russian's little eyes gleamed as he watched Breese nervously moving to go. "Yes, I suppose you won't need me. As a matter of fact, I was thinking of taking the six o'clock boat to Key West tonight. I suppose I'd better get back to the hotel and pack. Yes, I'd better pack. I haven't much time." He fumbled with his watch.

"But surely you're not going before the funeral?" the Russian inquired blandly.

"I'm afraid I'll have to," he coughed nervously. "I wasn't sure of staying anyway. I'm afraid I'm not up to it." Then he caught himself up: "Besides, there won't be a funeral here. Take the body to New York for the family vault. Rice will look after that." He paused, and licked his lips. "My son-in-law, you say?" He shook his head. "I can't understand it. I don't know what Mary'll say. She's all in. Can't talk. I'd better go to the hotel."

He moved for the door. But Smith stopped him.

"There's just one formality you'll have to go through with," the detective informed him. "Your wife's will is going to be read this afternoon at Mr. Brennon's office. I believe he was her attorney here. And he especially asked me to have all of you there."

Breese fumbled with his stick.

"Her will? Oh, yes. But I've got to get back to New York."

"It won't take long," Smith assured him. "You can still make that boat tonight."

"Very well—very well," Breese repeated, his hand at the door. "I'll do that."

Smith watched the old man stumble nervously out of the room. Then he turned to the Russian who now smiled triumphantly at him.

"Damned if there isn't something in it," Smith muttered.

CHAPTER XIV
THE WILL OF MRS. BREESE

MR. CHARLES BRENNON, HAVANA representative of several important New York law firms, maintained his offices in the older quarters of the city. Here the streets were so exceedingly narrow that walking became an adventure and riding a miracle. Decrepit buildings rose in medieval gloom from the congested street and the crumbling rock pile that housed Mr. Brennon was distinguished by being the most decrepit of them all.

We found it with some difficulty, for both name and number had been erased by time. But a kindly café proprietor several doors away pointed out the building after we had refreshed ourselves at his bar with cocoanut milk properly iced and sweetened, a soft drink delicacy that was a favorite with Perutkin.

As we came through the ancient arch of Mr. Brennon's building, we were accosted by a whining old man who waved a pad of blue tickets in our faces. He was one of the numerous lottery peddlers who infest the gullible city. Smith waved him aside but the Russian called him back and demanded a sheaf of tickets.

"I have a feeling," exclaimed Perutkin, "that a great vein of luck has seized me. There is light upon this case, and light in my soul." He pocketed the blue lottery paper. "I shall be both famous and rich. Then I shall be truly miserable!" he sighed mournfully.

Even Smith could not help laughing at the vagaries of the man. The three of us stepped gingerly into a musty elevator cage and hoped for the best. Slowly the old man in charge tugged us up the narrow shaft. On the third floor we were deposited directly in front of Mr. Brennon's dim suite of offices. As we entered the ante-room the smell of antiquity overpowered us. From the rug that had long since lost all semblance of its rightful color and the mottled melancholy walls to the white-whiskered office boy at his dust-laden desk, the room seemed to have been transported out of a bygone age. To judge from the dimly seen pictures on the wall, the world had stopped with the Spanish-American war. Mr. Brennon, as I discovered later, was one of those Americans who had come to Cuba to fight and had been conquered by the dolorous quality of the country. So there were photographs and woodcuts of the patriots of independence, scenes of the sinking of the Maine, a wash drawing of Roosevelt at San Juan and a brown faded memento of Mr. Brennon's own company, grouped fiercely around their commander.

Smith had insisted that we come earlier than the rest because he wanted the opportunity of an uninterrupted interview with the lawyer.

While the white-whiskered office boy went forth to announce us to Mr. Brennon, I reminded the detective that the elder Breese had been the first to mention the subject of a will when he summoned us to his suite to warn us against the actor.

"I haven't forgotten," said Smith.

"What would you think," intervened the Russian, "if, when we hear the will read, we discover that Mr. Thomas inherits the entire estate?"

"I'd say it would look bad for Thomas," Smith replied.

"And if Mr. Breese proves a false prophet? If Mr. Thomas receives nothing?"

"Then," said Smith, "we'll be more at sea than ever."

"No," said the Russian. "You will have convincing proof that Mr. Breese deliberately lied to implicate the actor, which is what I have maintained all along."

But here the white-whiskered office boy returned with Mr. Brennon. Although it was almost unbearably hot, the old lawyer affected a high-wing collar and a rather shiny but undeniably substantial morning coat. He was well over seventy, with silver mustachios and his faded blue eyes smiled feebly at us. He met us with a quavering flow of welcome—he hailed from somewhere in Tennessee—and he seemed to take it as his own short-sightedness that we had come a half-hour too soon. Certainly the old man and his establishment were not easily reconciled with Mrs. Breese, who had been as modern as this morning's newspaper put out upon the streets the night before.

He asked us into his private office, mustier, if possible, than his ante-room. He moved feebly but with the dignity of an old soldier. After reassuring himself that we were comfortable, he retired into the folds of his own armchair and waited for the detective to begin inquiry.

"I shall be very glad to tell you what I can," he said, after Smith had made known his mission. "Of course, you understand I cannot divulge the contents of the will until the proper time. But I dare say you won't press me on that. I expect to read it in half an hour. Now—" he cleared his throat, and one gnarled hand played with a yellow ivory pen-holder—"you ask me the circumstances that led Mrs. Breese to make this will. I can tell you only what I know.

"Some time ago—to be exact, shortly after that very unfortunate divorce action—" he shook his head mournfully—"an unhappy lady, Mrs. Breese. Dreadful tragedy." He looked off and then seemed to collect his thoughts. "But, as I was saying, shortly after her divorce trial, Mrs. Breese consulted Henry O'Brien in New York. Mrs. Breese asked Mr. O'Brien to write her will. Unfortunately, just as Mr. O'Brien set to work, Mrs. Breese said she must leave for Havana. So Mr. O'Brien very kindly suggested that I attend to the will when she got here. I received a letter from him to that effect.

"I waited for Mrs. Breese to come here, but she didn't. So I took it upon myself to call on her, and she received me, and we had a very interesting talk. I made out the will. I really had very little to do with it. I was unfamiliar with Mrs. Breese or her family, and I merely took down what she dictated and had my clerks sign as witnesses." He paused. "I think that's all I know, gentlemen, and I'm sure I'll be delighted if it can be of any help to you."

"Then we are to understand," inquired Smith, "that Mrs. Breese was not particularly anxious to make out a will? That she only did so because you suggested it?"

"I had my instructions from Mr. O'Brien," the lawyer explained.

Smith nodded. "That's a very important point," he explained. "If Mrs. Breese made out a will a week ago under someone's influence—someone connected with her establishment—we would want to know that. It might be a very important factor."

"As far as I know, gentlemen," the lawyer said, "Mrs. Breese made her will under no undue influence. No one was with her when I called first, or when she signed the document here in my office in the presence of my clerks."

The white-whiskered office boy (I later learned that he had been his employer's bugler in the war) announced Gordon Rice's arrival. Mr. Brennon instructed that the promoter be shown in at once.

Rice greeted us briskly. He seemed to regard the forthcoming ceremony as an event of no particular importance and he fumed at the tardiness of the others.

"Main thing I'm interested in," he confided, "is to find out if Mrs. Breese made any special request for the funeral. It's going to be a sad business, that. And it's up to me to take care of it. The children aren't up to it, and Mr. Breese is just about all in. I want to get him off to the States as fast as possible."

The Russian looked up significantly at Smith, but the detective made no comment.

Then the aged office boy ushered the actor in. For the occasion, Mr. Thomas had donned conservative blue flannels, black shoes, a pale blue shirt, and a black four-in-hand. He wove his mourning into the ensemble. His expression was slightly defiant as he looked at us.

No one spoke after the actor entered. Mr. Brennon began turning over long sheets of paper, and examining them through his thick glasses. The Russian mopped his red face, for the room was stifling hot.

It was fully ten minutes before the elder Breese was announced. He was accompanied by the Countess and his son. Mr. Breese seemed to have recovered somewhat from his agitation. Something of his habitual hardness had returned to his expression and he was quite curt with us.

The Countess was dressed in black, and because she had been annoyed by persistent news photographers, her white, haggard face was swathed in a heavy veil. Her brown eyes seemed unnaturally large and bright.

Her brother, who followed her in, took his place carefully away from the rest of us. He, too, showed signs of the emotional shock he had undergone, and he smoked many cigarettes while we waited for the lawyer to begin. I noticed that he looked at the actor but once and then with obvious hatred.

There was a stiff restrained silence for a moment.

The old lawyer had spread the will before him. "It is my duty," he quavered, "to read you the last will and testament of the late Dora Huntington Breese."

He paused and brought the document closer to his thick glasses. Then he plunged into the usual formula of Mrs. Breese's soundness of mind at the time the will was composed. The first few paragraphs disposed of several bequests to favorite servants. Five thousand dollars was given the Association for the Reform of Marriage—of which I had never heard—and sums in proportion to the Speyer Home for Animals, the Society for Psychical Research, the Juilliard Foundation and the Girl Scouts of America. Surely, a strange coupling of movements!

The lawyer read on tremulously. I took notes of the will, and I found my pencil making comments upon what I had heard. Thus I wrote: "*To my daughter, the Countess Giering-Trelovitch, I leave the income of a trust fund ... three hundred thousand dollars for life ... on condition that the said trust fund revert to the estate should she resume relationship in any way, shape, manner or form, with her divorced husband, the Count Giering-Trelovitch.*"

I saw Smith look at the Russian. I know that in my note-book I wrote: "Indirect motive for the Count! Mrs. Breese hated him, and the antagonism was undoubtedly mutual!"

"*To Guy Thomas, I bequeath the income of seventy-five thousand dollars in trust as an expression of my gratitude for his loyal friendship and companionship. Should Mr. Thomas remarry, this trust fund will revert to the estate.*"

The actor looked up, puzzled, and disappointed, I think. I find in my note-book: "Breese lied about the will. Score one for the Russian!" Then, as I looked at my notes of the Thomas portion of the estate my eye caught the word "remarry." I wrote: "Investigate. Mr. Thomas is a bachelor. Did Mrs. Breese propose marrying him when she made out the will? Evidently."

The actor's exact status after he arrived in Havana had never been plain to me. Mrs. Breese first announced her engagement to him on board the yacht. After her son's attempt at suicide, she had apparently recanted. Then she had changed her mind once more. And yet, if Thomas' own story were true, she accepted without protest his plan to marry a New York chorus girl, and even proposed financing the venture.

"*To my first husband, Henry Breese, I leave no reproaches but an earnest entreaty not to subject another woman to the suffering he has caused me.*"

I saw the old man wince, and the Countess turn toward him, as if to comfort him.

Henry Breese, Jr., received the residuary estate. As executor, Mrs. Breese named her "*loyal friend, Gordon Rice, and I implore my children to show him the same obedience and respect that they would give their own father were he worthy of it.*"

Another blow at the elder Breese! Seemingly the antagonism, at least, on Mrs. Breese's side, was even more deep-rooted than I had suspected.

Then followed the strangest portion of this strange document:

"*Three days after my death, when it is established that life cannot possibly return to my body, I desire that my body be burned and cremated. The ashes are to be placed in a suitable urn and brought on board the yacht Mary Rose, no matter where it may be docked, at my death. At the hour of midnight my ashes are to be scattered into the sea. There are to be no prayers, no music and no flowers. The ceremonial is to be carried out exactly as I have instructed. I have never been free in my stay upon earth, and in the life hereafter I want nothing more than to ride the seven seas, my soul as free as the winds.*"

CHAPTER XV
WEATHER PREDICTION

SMITH AND I LOOKED at each other incredulously. But later I reasoned that the melodramatic exit Mrs. Breese had elected was entirely in keeping. Even in death Mrs. Breese wanted to make news of herself. I could picture her dictating her lurid wishes to the old lawyer and relishing his amazement. I am convinced that she regarded the will as essentially meaningless. She probably thought she would change it a half-dozen times before she was done playing with the prospect of death.

Then the lawyer was done. No one spoke. I realized the Countess had risen, and her brother. They left the room without a word. The elder Breese whispered something to Rice, who nodded, and then joined his children.

"When," the actor cleared his throat and addressed the lawyer with grave dignity, "when do you plan to file this will in the Surrogate's court?"

"Immediately," replied the lawyer.

"No hurry, is there?" demanded Smith sharply. But the actor did not deign to reply. He took up his gloves and stick and stalked out of the room.

We emerged into the dingy corridor once more. Neither Smith nor the Russian made any comment upon the ceremony that had just been concluded. Once out of the building, we clambered aboard a lumbering street car. A native motorman who smoked loathsomely heavy cigarettes sent our car clanging through the narrow street. Heavily rouged and bejewelled matrons sat side by side, with grimy day laborers about us preempting the shady side.

Every so often a bullet-headed negro boy would run through the car crying the virtues of his bags of hot peanuts. Our route took us past several cemeteries and the motorman would lift his cap to a passing cortège, flick his cigarette and then clang forward more noisily than ever.

"You see," shouted the Russian in my ear above the clamor of the car, "other mortals may be dismissed as easily as all this, with the lifting of the cap, but Mrs. Breese wanted more out of death! What a fool! But I look forward to her funeral! I shall enjoy it!" He laughed heartily. "I have always enjoyed funerals. They are such a commentary on the unimportance of life!"

Smith looked at him nastily, for the Russian was shocking his staid sensibilities.

All unconscious of this, Perutkin continued for all to hear:

"For my own funeral, I require nothing but a hole in the ground, and flowers. Many flowers. I wish to smell sweet in death. Not that that is possible. Quite the contrary. But at least civilized man can give superficial beauty even to decay. And he should do so. I am all in favor of civilization. The more the better."

The rest of his somewhat disconnected philosophy on funerals was lost in the business of leaping out of the street car, for the motorman never waited the convenience of his passengers, and we almost rode past the ornamental police headquarters. We accompanied Smith to his office. While we waited patiently, he sat down at his desk and began typing strenuously. When he was done, he said:

"I've often found it useful, when a case gets to this stage of the game, to write down the known facts and see how they jibe. Now you two know this case as well as I do. I want you to look this over and see what I've missed."

The Russian and I glanced over his shoulder, and we read:

"*Thomas*—bad egg—was in the house when Mrs. Breese was killed—engaged to her, forged check which was discovered—had another girl—is mentioned in will as next husband—yet Thomas insists Mrs. Breese didn't mind his marrying other girl and was paying him for his 'loyalty' during divorce trial. Thomas possessed revolver and knew how to use it.

"*Breese, Sr.*—had access to house. May have been there on night of murder. Hated his wife and was hated by her. Evidently lied when he said wife was making will in favor of Thomas. Evidently wanted Thomas accused of murder. Now anxious to get away.

"*The Count*—in Mrs. Breese's bad books, who had been keeping her daughter away from him, and wanted him to stay away even after her death. Is suspected of one murder. He has confessed and disappeared. Was in the house at the time.

"*Mary Rose Breese*—judging from mother's will, wanted to return to her divorced husband. Was in the house at the time.

"*Henry Breese, Jr.*—Violently hated the actor. Violently opposed his marrying his mother. Once owned revolver. Was in the house at the time. Inherits bulk of the estate."

"You omit Gordon Rice, I see," exclaimed the Russian.

"I omitted him purposely," said Smith. "He's got a perfectly good alibi, and no motive."

"And yet," said the Russian meditatively, "Rice knows something."

"How do you get that?" inquired Smith.

"The feeling is intangible," explained the Russian. "But to one who is sensitive to human beings—I am very sensitive—that is why I am a great detective—but to one like myself there is something about Rice that needs clarifying. I have that curious feeling that he is holding something back." He paused. "Are you sure about his alibi?"

"Sure?" exclaimed Smith. "I've got the word of the American Minister himself that Rice spent the entire evening at his house! They were together all the time, except for five minutes. I talked to the clerk who saw and heard him telephone. You wouldn't want a better alibi than that?"

"No," said the Russian. "Did you, by any chance, ask the clerk what Mr. Rice said over the telephone?"

"No, I didn't," said Smith. "What difference would it make?"

"None at all," replied the Russian. "I was just curious. However, granted that Rice could not have committed the murder—he was not at the scene of the crime—but isn't it strange to you that both Rice and Breese should hammer at you to arrest the actor? Isn't it strange that Rice should bring you the telegram from the detective agency, hired by Breese, to find out what they could about the actor? What must we conclude? Especially in view of the case against Breese? Only this: Rice is anxious to protect Breese."

"Well, maybe," conceded Smith.

"Undoubtedly!" insisted the Russian. "I shall go one step further. Let us consider the history of this case: After Mrs. Breese's divorce, Mr. Rice scorned her husband, whom he had known for many years, and sided with the lady. Is that natural? No. Men do not break friendship under such circumstances. And behold: When Mrs. Breese is dead, the two men are friends openly once more. What does that suggest to you? Remember, Breese was anxious for a reconciliation. To me it suggests that the two men only pretended to quarrel during the divorce trial. Rice sided with Mrs. Breese so as to be in a position to influence her. That's why he so violently opposed her marriage to the actor. Remember, he did not intend marrying her himself. There was no question of love between this man and the woman. What then was his motive in coming down here with her and campaigning so strenuously against the actor? Obviously, he wanted her to remarry his friend Breese.

"Now, mark this—Breese calls you to his hotel before the murder and warns you against the actor. Rice comes to the house, after the murder, and the first thing he does is to accuse the actor. He produces telegrams from the detective agency (hired by Breese) and tells you about the forged check. I hold no brief for the actor, but I don't think he forged that check. I think Breese did himself. But observe how in every development of the case Breese and Rice work together, and yet apart—what does that suggest?"

"Do you mean to say that Rice took part in the murder, or knew about it beforehand?" Smith asked skeptically.

"No," said the Russian. "I believe Breese unburdened himself to his friend after the murder, threw himself upon Rice's mercy, and Rice has been doing everything he can to save his friend. And if in the process the actor gets hurt why, I should think that Rice would be the type to accept such a miscarriage of justice with the comforting reflection that Mr. Thomas would get only what he deserved."

"For that matter," replied Smith, "I can build up the same case against you!"

"Against me?" exclaimed the Russian.

"Certainly," said Smith. "You are protecting your friend, the Count. He was not only in the house at the time of the murder, but he actually confessed to it, after consulting you. You have been hammering away on old man Breese. Why? If I use the same logic you do, I could say—to protect your friend."

The Russian laughed. "You have me there, Mr. Smith," he admitted admiringly. "It had never occurred to me. But you're not serious?"

"No," said Smith. "I'm not serious about any theories. And this case seems to me to consist of nothing else. I'm looking for something definite, something tangible."

The Russian picked up Smith's summary and studied it once more.

"There are many definite, tangible things here," he replied, "but they are of little value—at present. I notice you have marked down the Breese children. I admit they should be watched, as a matter of routine. But I would safely pass them for the moment. Our main target right now is the father. Concentrate upon him, my friend!"

"You're at it again!" said Smith.

"Besides," I put in, "old man Breese is leaving for the States on the six o'clock boat, isn't he?"

Smith shook his head. "No, Mr. Breese's landing card is going to be questioned when he gets to Key West and he'll have to return to Havana to straighten it out. I've got that arranged. I'm not taking any chances of losing anybody in this case."

"Good!" approved the Russian heartily. He planted his panama firmly upon his huge head. "If I recall rightly, the funeral is to take place three days after the lady's death—tomorrow at midnight, to be exact." Smith nodded. "What is the weather prediction for tomorrow?"

"The weather prediction?" Smith repeated puzzled.

"Yes," said the Russian. "Examine that copy of the Havana Post which you keep so neatly folded upon the desk. What does it say?"

Smith glanced obediently at the paper, evidently humoring the Russian. "Let me see——" he found the weather column. "Storms," he read.

"But that is magnificent!" shouted the Russian. He snatched the paper rudely from the detective. "Let me see. I cannot believe it. Yes, it is true! Storms!"

Smith stared at him, open-mouthed.

The Russian swept his hat from his head in one violent gesture and flung it upon the desk.

"To work!" he cried. "To work, my friends."

Then he chuckled. "Of course, you do not understand? You do not see the connection. I am, perhaps, premature. What if there should be no storms? No, I shall wait." He regained the panama and once more it was squeezed down upon his head. "Tomorrow we go to the funeral, invited or not. And, my friends"—he was already moving to the door—"pray for storms, my friends, pray for storms!"

CHAPTER XVI
THE FUNERAL AT MIDNIGHT

THE FUNERAL PARTY ASSEMBLED upon the ill-lit dock at eleven o'clock that night. Although the moon was shrouded, there were no signs of the prophesied storm. The black and green waters of the Bay rippled gently, and only the mildest of tropical breezes swept past us. Far off we could see the *Mary Rose* riding gracefully at anchor, her lights twinkling invitingly to the desolate dock. Occasionally a tug shrieked its warning and plowed off to its berth.

Funerals are never pleasant affairs for me, and this one, with all its attendant circumstances, brought an involuntary shiver as I waited impatiently for the yacht's launches. Faces of the mourners were hardly distinguishable. Vaguely I knew that the group of four nearby, whispering softly among themselves, were the Breese family and Gordon Rice. At some considerable distance the shadow of the actor paced up and down.

Neither Smith nor the Russian had arrived yet. I could expect anything of Perutkin, but I knew that Smith was a model of punctuality and I wondered what had detained him. His instructions to me that evening were somewhat enigmatical. I could not help feeling that for the first time since the case started he was withholding something of import.

Black figures glided past us—sailors and watchmen and all the dark crew of the dock, leaving or arriving at their posts. From far off we heard the melancholy crooning of a native love-song, punctuated by the harsh monotonous twanging of a guitar.

I heard Rice say aloud: "What's the matter with that launch? It's late." These were the first words above a whisper that I had heard from any of the four since my arrival.

But Rice fell silent once more. I lit a match and consulted my watch. Then I looked toward the yacht once more and it seemed to me that the wind had risen. The waters below us began to swirl. I saw the *Mary Rose* rock spasmodically. Rice looked up at the dark sky. He muttered something under his breath.

Then we heard a taxi, and I could descry the figure of Smith rushing toward us. He apologized hurriedly for his tardiness, and was relieved to find that the launch had not yet started out.

"Where's the Russian?" I asked.

"He'll be around," Smith said vaguely. Then he took a police whistle from his pocket and gave three shrill blasts. An answering siren from the yacht responded, as if the signal had been prearranged. Then we heard the faint chugging of the launch, growing steadily louder in our ears, and we could make out its shadowy outline as it chopped the angry waters.

Without a word, the funeral party permitted itself to be helped aboard the launch by the crew of two. Smith and I were the last ones to leave the dock. The motor roared anew. I saw Rice looking up at the sky.

"We'd better hurry," he said. "This looks like a real storm coming."

"Oh, no," said Smith reassuringly. "Just a bit of rain. I've lived around here for five years and I know a real storm when I see one."

I saw one of the sailors at his motor wink sardonically to the other at this.

"Well, if there is a storm," said Rice, "we're going to turn back. Have to postpone it."

"No," said Breese. "Don't want to do that. I've got to go home tomorrow."

Rice looked doubtfully at him. But by this time the launch had drawn up alongside the *Mary Rose*, and we clambered out as best we could. The group of four proceeded immediately to the music-room, followed, at some distance, by the actor. Smith and I paced the deck.

After a moment's silence, Smith said, looking about carefully to make sure that he was not overheard: "I'm expecting things to happen tonight."

I felt a curious tingling of excitement. I begged for some inkling of his plans. But Smith shook his head.

"Only thing for you to do is to wait and watch. No matter what happens, don't worry."

I heard footsteps behind us, and I swung around quickly. I gaped at Perutkin—in the half light—a new Perutkin, resplendent in morning coat and top-hat and white gloves that almost gleamed silver in the night. In one hand he held a gold-tipped stick, which he swung with a swagger.

"All is ready," he announced.

As if the yacht were awaiting his command, I heard the heavy rattle of chains as the anchor was drawn up. Then the engines throbbed and the dock receded.

We heard the deafening peal of thunder that makes a tropical storm so frightful. Lightning raced across the black sky. The yacht rose upon the waves, and we felt a sudden drenching rain upon our faces. We beat a hasty retreat to the cabin corridor for protection.

I heard the Russian chuckling, and as he came into the corridor, he pointed to the pouring sky.

"My partner!" he cried. I could only stare at him, puzzled. A member of the crew darted past us. We heard him slamming the deck doors and battering them shut.

"Time to see the Captain," Smith said. He was as puzzling to me as was the Russian.

"Yes," chuckled the Russian. "You'll find him an excellent fellow. I've been dining very well with him. He'll coöperate, I assure you."

Smith nodded and left us. The Russian paced up and down, rubbing his hands delightedly, looking at me with a playful grin and chuckling in high good humor. His smile did not leave him when he saw Rice emerge from the music-room, a frown upon his ordinarily placid face.

"We'll have to turn back," Rice said to me. "It's a bad enough business for the family without this storm."

"But, surely," said the Russian, "you will not disobey the strict injunctions of Mrs. Breese. It was, so to speak, her dying wish. Three days after her death she specified."

"Mrs. Breese," retorted Rice, "wouldn't want to make her family and friends miserable. She didn't know about this storm."

"It would look very bad in the newspapers," the Russian shook his head doubtfully. He turned to me, "Don't you think so?" And before I could reply, "But why do I ask? We have just been discussing that," he lied glibly, "and you yourself made that point."

"I can't help it," snapped Rice. "We're turning back."

He strode past us. When he had gone, the Russian laughed.

"And I would be willing to wager that we are not," he said.

But whatever the private joke of the Russian (which Smith evidently shared) I could not quite appreciate its humor. The yacht rolled unmercifully, and although I am a fairly good sailor, I do not enjoy being pitched about. Outside, the wind assumed the proportions, it seemed to me, of a cyclone, although the Russian laughed at the comparison.

"Why, this is excellent weather!" he exclaimed cheerfully, sitting down upon the leather bench beside me, and holding his top-hat carefully against his breast. "A little blow like this means nothing—nothing at all."

The ship's lights blinked in my eyes as the fury of the storm increased. I saw Smith carefully making his way down the stairs toward us.

"Well?" said the Russian.

Smith nodded, with an air of self-satisfaction.

"Mr. Rice wants to turn back," said the Russian.

"I know," said Smith. "He's still with the Captain. But it seems there are reasons why the Captain can't follow orders. Rice thinks the skipper's crazy." Smith grinned exasperatingly.

Another peal of thunder rolled in the sky, and through the windows I was startled by the accompanying flash of lighting.

"This may be a joke on us, at that," said Smith, blinking.

"Nonsense!" retorted the Russian. "Rest easy, my friend. Everything is working famously."

Rice stumbled down the stairs, clutching the banister. When he reached our landing, I could see his face was purple.

"Go up there and argue with that madman!" he shouted at Smith. "He won't turn back!"

"I've already done that," Smith shrugged his shoulders. "But I wouldn't worry, Mr. Rice. This boat can stand a heavier storm than this." He drew out his cheap watch. "It's ten minutes to twelve. Don't you think you'd better summon the family to the deck for the ceremony?"

Rice didn't reply, but staggered to the first door, opened it, and then banged it behind him.

"Excellent!" exclaimed the Russian. "We need very little now."

He stopped short, as the dapper figure of the Captain came down the stairs toward us. He was in his forties, with the sharp eye of the adventurer not uncommon in yacht skippers, and with none of the ponderous dignity that goes with commanders burdened with the responsibility of larger craft. His blue eyes twinkled merrily as he greeted Smith.

"All's well," he chuckled. Apparently he was part of the conspiracy, too. I felt somewhat chagrined that a mere stranger had intervened in a case in which I felt a proprietary interest.

"You won't regret it, Captain," Smith replied.

The door opened, and Rice emerged. In his arms he clutched a blue urn. Here were the ashes of Mrs. Breese. The strange funeral party stumbled after him—the elder Breese, his daughter, very white and seemingly dazed, young Breese and the actor.

The Captain bared his head. Smith tugged at the door to the deck. The wind howled in our ears. The mourners stumbled forward. Rice clutched his burden spasmodically.

A driving rain beat our faces. The night was pitch black now. I heard the door slam behind us. I heard Perutkin's voice boom out:

"He, who has the ashes of Dora Breese, murdered by a fiend, unknown, will now cast them into the sea, as she desired!"

I shivered involuntarily. I thought I heard a moan in the wind. Then there was a splash. The Countess cried out. She was near me. Smith opened the door hurriedly and as hurriedly the mourners stumbled to shelter. The strange funeral was over.

Wringing wet, we chattered, as if in relief. Rice conducted the elder Breese and the children back to the warmth of the music-room, where an open fire blazed. The actor, impervious to the chill in Rice's eyes, stumbled after them.

"Now," said the Russian, "come with me, gentlemen." He included me in his gesture of invitation.

We followed him down the long corridor to the cabins. I fell against the wall intermittently, for the rocking of the boat grew more violent, and the wind howled so that the very timbers rattled.

We paused before the first cabin. The Russian knocked loudly at the door. A voice bade us enter. The Russian flung the door open.

A very pale young man greeted us.

"Now," said the Russian, "we are complete."

The Count Giering-Trelovitch advanced toward us.

"Into the music-room with you, my friend," the Russian said harshly to the man who had confessed. "Join the others! Come!"

Without a word, the young man followed. I could see by Smith's expression that the advent of the Count was as much of a surprise to him as it was to me.

"You see," said Perutkin to the detective, "I have kept my word. I have produced him for you. It is only fair."

Whatever else he said was lost in a convulsive shiver of the boat. The lights dimmed and flashed crazily. Then suddenly we were plunged in darkness. I heard a woman's scream.

CHAPTER XVII
STORM

IN MY MEMORY I have a terribly vivid picture of the first few stifling moments in that black room. There was a scurrying of feet about me, confused shouts. Someone prodded me in the back so that I gasped for breath. Then the voice of Perutkin booming forth: "Quiet, everybody, quiet!" It was as if a schoolmaster were reproving a group of noisy children. For the next moment hushed silence reigned.

There was the barely audible click of metal, and the Russian played the weak rays of a flash-light upon the wall. But it served only to illuminate his own stern visage, curiously ominous under the black top-hat. He seemed an unearthly figure out of a dream. That he was conscious of the effect he produced I cannot doubt. He had a Russian sense of personal drama.

"There is nothing to fear!" he said slowly, but his voice belied his words. "You are all safe. Something's wrong with the electric plant, and it will undoubtedly be repaired in a moment."

"There's been something wrong with this boat ever since we got on," I heard the elder Breese's voice tremble. I could not see his face. He was one of many shadows among us. "Where's the Captain?"

"Yes——" this now with Rice's voice. "Bring him down here. You with the flash-light, I told him to turn back. Why didn't he?"

"I shall bring the Captain," the Russian promised. "But again I tell you, there is nothing to fear."

He moved to the door, the light traveling uncannily with him. Then the door closed, and once more we were plunged in darkness.

"I've never had such an experience in all my life," I heard the actor complaining fatuously. "Hang it all, this is a funny way of running a boat."

"Shut up, can't you?" barked Rice. "Does somebody know where we are?"

"All I can tell you," Smith responded placidly, "is that we're out of sight of land. But we can't be far from the coast." The yacht heaved and shadows toppled. I heard Rice swear. Smith muttered to me: "This is a real storm all right. It had me fooled. I thought it'd pass over."

The boat creaked and rattled, and the engines throbbed as if in struggle.

Then the door opened, and Perutkin appeared with his flash-light. It was good to be rid of the dark again.

"I'm sorry," he announced, "but the Captain can tell me nothing." He paused. "Nothing!"

"What the devil do you mean by that?" demanded the elder Breese. "Where is he? Bring him down here. I'll have him fired the minute we land."

"That is your affair, Mr. Breese," replied the Russian, playing the light full upon the face of the financier. "I know nothing of that. All I can tell you is that the Captain cannot come down here. He is not leaving the bridge."

"What's wrong with the lights?" asked Rice.

"They are investigating now," replied the Russian. "They do not know themselves." He set his flash-light upon the table, so that it shed its faint rays upon us all. "Meanwhile we must content ourselves with this. It will do in an emergency."

"It's outrageous!" cried the actor. "It's never happened before."

"Where are we?" demanded Rice, straining to see out of the window.

"That I cannot tell you," responded the Russian. "They were not very communicative—your officers. The Captain growled at me as if he would bite me, and the first officer was not very polite either." He stopped short, as the Countess rose from the sofa and stared at a shadowy figure in one corner. It was with some effort that she stifled a scream.

The Count came forward. For the first time his presence was revealed to the mourners.

"Where on earth did you come from?" Rice gasped at the intruder.

The actor seemed to have gone mad. "Somebody arrest him! Somebody arrest him!" he shouted. "Here, you detectives—here he is!"

"Quiet!" roared Perutkin.

"I must apologize to you, Mary," the Count began quietly. "And to you, gentlemen. I did not come here to startle you. The fact is, I came on board to give myself up."

"Then sit down!" commanded Perutkin. "Consider yourself under arrest, and when we land we shall know what to do with you."

The Count nodded, and quietly seated himself in a corner, almost out of sight of the others in the pale light. The Countess averted her eyes. I saw her deliberately turn to gaze, expressionless, at Smith, standing in the opposite corner, although I am sure she did not see him.

"Well," said Rice, still staring at the Count, "this is quite a shock to me. How did you get on the boat?"

"No one stopped me," replied the Count. "I'm sorry I have disturbed you."

"What's this about a confession?" asked Rice. "Do you mean to tell me that you murdered Mrs. Breese?"

"Yes," replied the Count. "I did."

"But in the name of Heaven, why?" demanded Rice. "I'd like to know. I'd like to know why anyone would kill Dora Breese—one of the finest women that ever lived. I'd like to know how an apparently decent young chap like you could do a fiendish thing like that."

"Is it so unlikely?" demanded the Count. "Didn't you believe I was guilty of murder in Riga?"

"I did not!" snapped Rice. "I told Dora she had you all wrong. But, of course, she was right. You couldn't fool her." He stopped, overwhelmed. "God, I can't believe it!" he muttered. "It doesn't seem real."

"If you don't mind," said the Count wearily, "I'd rather not discuss it."

But here Perutkin intervened. "Do you know, Mr. Rice, I agree with you. It doesn't seem real. I don't think my friend's confession is worth this——" he snapped his fingers. "He's being a fool, that's all."

"But why?" demanded Rice. "Why does he confess? That's what gets me!"

"I shall tell you," said Perutkin. "He thinks he is being chivalrous. He thinks he is doing something noble. He does not realize he is merely obstructing justice." He swung suddenly on the Countess who was looking at him intently. "You, Madame, you do not believe him? You were his wife. You know him."

"I don't know what to believe," the girl said desperately.

"And you, young man——" He turned to the younger Breese—"what do you think?"

The boy squirmed in the chair, but said nothing.

"And you?" He advanced slowly upon the elder Breese. "Have you any opinions on the matter, sir?"

"I don't know anything about it!" snapped Breese. "Let me alone."

But his son sprang up. "What's the use of this? Of course he didn't do it. You know who did it, and I do, too. It's that cad over there—yes, you——" he blazed at Thomas. "You can't fool me!"

"Hang it all, stop it!" shrieked the actor. "This is getting on my nerves. I can't stand it any more. I really can't."

"You must have proof for such grave charges," Perutkin intervened solemnly. "What proof have you?"

"I don't need any proof," shouted the boy. "Look at him. Isn't that enough? If it weren't for him, Mother would be alive today. He ruined her life. He killed her. And he's not going to get away with it either!"

Rice reached for the boy to calm him. Young Breese, on the verge of tears, tried to draw away.

"Go ahead! Say anything you want!" challenged the actor. "I was your mother's friend. Why don't you look at her will? She says there what she thinks of me! I did everything in the world for her. And all the thanks I get is—this!" He swallowed piteously. "Hang it all, it isn't fair!"

"What in life is fair?" reflected the Russian gravely. "We are none of us appreciated, Mr. Thomas. But you believe that the Count is guilty?"

"You've got his own word for it, haven't you?" countered the actor. "What do you want from me? A man comes to you and says he's a murderer, and you don't want to believe him. Of course! You'd rather believe *I* did it. I know you're all against me. But you'd better be careful—some of you! There's such a thing as libel. I've got lawyers to protect me!"

The door opened, and a harassed-looking wireless operator stumbled forward. His earnest, long face was white with fear and his steel spectacles quivered on his long, thin nose.

"Mr. Breese!" he called.

"Yes? Have you a message for me?"

"Yes, sir." But the operator made no move. He shifted uncomfortably from one foot to the other.

"Well, where is it?" demanded Breese finally.

"I haven't got it, exactly, sir—I——"

"What the devil do you mean?" growled the financier.

"Sir, I was about to take it—it was for you—but something went wrong with the set. I don't know yet what happened. I worked as fast as I could. Then I went out to see if the aerial had been damaged. And—it had. Cut through. And then, when I came back, I found the set smashed to pieces, as if someone with a hammer had just banged up everything. I reported to the Captain, sir, and he just sent word for me to report to you."

"Someone deliberately smashed your set?" Breese looked at him incredulously. "But who would do a thing like that?"

"I can't understand it, sir. It's never happened to me before."

The radio man blinked uncomfortably. Tiny beads of perspiration stood out upon his narrow forehead.

"No use going into that now," Rice said. "He'd better get to work and start repairs. Dangerous business being without radio in this storm."

"Yes, sir, it is," agreed the operator. "I'll get right to work, sir. I've got some extra equipment. I'll see what I can do."

"That is very strange," said Perutkin as he left. "First someone tampers with the lights. And now the wireless is smashed."

"Well, anything can happen in a storm," put in Smith.

"How can storm get into the wireless room?" Rice snorted impatiently.

"But who in the world would deliberately smash our wireless?" Smith persisted. "It doesn't seem possible."

"It doesn't seem possible," retorted Rice, "that this man"—pointing to the Count—"should deliberately walk on board this yacht to give himself up. Yet there he is. How and why I don't know—yet! Perhaps he's responsible. He's been skulking around this boat!"

"I assure you, sir," the Count replied, "I know nothing of wireless."

"It's damn funny," muttered Rice. "I'd have this investigated the moment we get in!"

"How much longer have we got to go?" asked Breese. "We seem to be taking hours!"

"In such a storm," said the Russian, "we must proceed cautiously."

But here the harassed-looking operator returned. He seemed shaken with puzzled fear.

"I can't understand it, sir," he cried at Breese. "When I got back, someone had stolen all my spare equipment. I've searched high and low for it."

"But this is strange!" exclaimed Perutkin. "Are you sure?"

"Sure?" muttered the operator. "I'm not sure of anything any more."

"Then," said the Russian, "there is a maniac aboard. I am reminded of the famous Sebastopol tragedy, where someone with a homicidal humor played just such tricks upon a small passenger boat. Utterly destroyed it. It is curious. Very curious."

"What are you talking about?" exploded Rice. "What maniac? We know who's on board."

"But—do we?" countered the Russian. "My friend, the Count, came here unseen. How do we know who else has come?"

"Hang it all, find him then!" shrieked the actor, who had been listening open-mouthed. "If there's a madman on board he'll kill us all!"

"It is very strange," persisted the Russian quietly. "But in the Sebastopol case, twenty-one men, women and children were drowned thus. He crippled the radio, knocked a tremendous hole in her side, and completely ruined the engines."

"But why?" asked Smith.

"For the maniacal delight of destruction," the Russian replied calmly.

"Here——" barked Rice. "What are you trying to do? Scare everybody? If there's anybody on board, the crew'll handle him fast enough."

"If they find him," said the Russian. "Maniacs are cunning."

"But you don't know there *is* a maniac!" shouted Rice. He stopped short. Outside we heard the smash of wood upon wood. Resounding blows. Then the wash of waves. Suddenly a growl of many voices, and one purple oath.

Perutkin hurried out. He was gone but a moment. When he returned he said gravely: "A curious accident! Our lifeboats have been washed overboard."

"But that's impossible!" exclaimed Rice.

"So I would think," agreed the Russian. "I observed today that both boats were lashed fast. What are we to conclude?"

"Conclude nothing!" cried Rice. "Get hold of the Captain. Let him search this boat from top to bottom. We'll find out soon enough who's been doing this!"

Even as he spoke I was conscious that the lulling hum of the engines had died out. There was an empty silence, while the boat still tossed.

"The engines have stopped!" announced the Russian. "Listen!"

"We—we must be coming in!" quavered Breese hopefully.

"We can't be coming in!" the Russian contradicted, looking out of the window. "I see no sight of land, no harbor. Nothing but water and darkness."

"Then what's he stopping for?" demanded Rice. "We're not moving. Those engines are dead."

"I'll find out!" volunteered the operator nervously. But Perutkin halted him.

"No, you shall wait here. I shall myself investigate. It is high time."

Reluctantly the operator watched him go. He shuffled into a chair and sat down, nervously twisting his stubby fingers. He seemed decidedly ill at ease as he looked about him.

A peal of thunder rolled over our heads. I shuddered, as if it were an ominous warning of disaster.

The yacht seemed to list and chairs slid. I clutched at the wall. I can only record my physical actions in that room. My mind, it seemed to me, was in a daze from the moment I had boarded the yacht.

Finally the Russian came back. He walked slowly, with head bowed. He shut the door carefully behind him.

"Gentlemen," he announced gravely, "it is my duty to tell you that we are in great peril!" He paused. "Our engines have stopped. Our wireless is hopelessly smashed. Our lifeboats have been washed overboard. The ship lists dangerously, and is leaking. We are in the grip of a terrific storm—gentlemen," he sank suddenly to his knees, "gentlemen, pray for your lives!"

CHAPTER XVIII
ONE OF YOU

PERUTKIN MADE THE SIGN of the cross, and lifted his voice in the chant of the Russian church. The melancholy litany seemed endless. I watched him in fascinated horror. The rest could not believe their eyes. Breese stumbled out through the door, calling incoherently for aid. But no answer came through the darkness. Someone shouted: "Lifebelts!" To me then the word meant nothing, nor to the rest of us, for we stood helplessly watching the top-hatted figure upon bended knee in the prayer we could not understand.

Then the Russian stopped, and he drew himself up to his full height. "In my own tongue, and in the prayer of my mother, I have confessed my sins," he said. "Now my heart is light. I can meet the Unknown without fear." Once more he made the sign of the cross.

"Stop it!" shrieked the actor. "Can't you do something—somebody? I don't want to die!" His voice died out in a wail.

"You are white, Mr. Thomas," said the Russian. "You shiver. You are afraid."

"Where's the Captain?" Breese demanded. "Bring him here at once!"

The yacht rolled maliciously and the old man seized a chair to steady himself.

"There is only one Captain now," responded the Russian gravely, "and Him I cannot bring. But He will come!"

Rice stepped forward. "Things cannot be as bad as you say. I know this boat. She's weathered worse storms than this!"

"Perhaps," said the Russian. "But this is her last storm. The sea is pouring into her. While we stand here, she is sinking. It is only a matter of minutes."

"I won't believe it until the Captain says so!" snapped Rice.

"Ask him!" challenged the Russian. "If you can find him in the dark." Then he raised his voice. "It is the wrath of God. One of you killed cunningly and now all of us must die. So it is written, my friends."

"You've gone mad!" cried Breese. "I'll get the Captain myself."

"I'll go with you," his son volunteered.

"There is no need!" The Russian raised his hand. "Look!"

He pointed to the window. The red and white glare of rockets flashed before our eyes.

"I shall read for you!" said the Russian. "S.O.S. S.O.S. We have no wireless. We have no lifeboats. We are summoning aid."

Breese stood still, staring at the window. He tottered to a chair.

"Well," said Smith slowly, "I guess you're right. I guess we're in for it!"

"Yes," muttered Rice. "I guess we are."

We were startled by a jangling discordant laugh, and then we saw the Count rise from his shadowed corner.

"Stop that!" barked Rice. "Be a man! Have some consideration for this lady!"

"I can't help it," cried the Count. "It is such delicious humor. That I should come on this yacht and—and——" Once more he gave way to hysterical laughter.

"Yes," chimed in Smith, "it's a great joke on me, too. I came on board to get the man that killed Mrs. Breese. It won't do me much good now if I get him." He seated himself in a chair and pulled his hat down over his eyes. "I only hope it comes fast. It's the waiting I mind."

"Maybe they'll see our signals," the wireless operator, who had been sitting unnoticed, suddenly burst forth.

"They'd signal back, wouldn't they?" demanded Smith.

"And there is no answer!" boomed the Russian. "Our eyes will close before we see the answer. We can do nothing, I tell you. We are in the hands of the Almighty."

He took from his pocket a thick black book. "When I went to see the Captain he could give me nothing but this—his Bible. It is not my Bible, but I shall pray for you all, miserable sinners. I shall pray for you all."

"Then pray to yourself!" cried Breese. "This isn't a revival meeting. Do you want to start a panic?"

"The burden of Tyre!" boomed the Russian. "Howl, ye ships of Tarshish; for it is laid waste, so that there is no house, no entering it: from the land of Chittim it is revealed to them."

Now Smith turned on the Russian. "Shut up!" he growled. "Get over there and pray if you want to—nobody else does."

"Confess your sins," the Russian intoned.

"Now, let's be sensible," said Smith. "We're in a bad way, and we all know it. It's not going to help matters if we lose our heads. Everybody keep quiet and wait."

"I don't want to die," wailed the actor.

"No, I guess you don't," said Smith drily, as the Russian droned on. "Too bad about the little girl waiting for you. I guess there'll be no trip to Paris." The actor groaned. "You were a bad actor and a bad egg, but I guess you're going to get all that's coming to any of us. And after you went to all that trouble—forging that check!"

"I didn't forge any check!" protested the actor.

Smith shrugged his shoulders. "What difference can it possibly make now?" he demanded. "I don't care if you did or not. I can't do anything about it. This case is out of my hands."

"But you've got to believe me," cried the actor.

"Yes, you can believe that, anyway." I started, as the younger Breese rose from his chair. "I—I forged that check, Mr. Smith."

"You?"

His father cried aghast: "What's come over you, son?"

"Oh, I'm not sorry about it," young Breese said bitterly. "But as long as things are the way they are, I might as well tell you the truth. I forged that check because I wanted to stop Mother from marrying him. I thought that would stop her."

"You shouldn't have done that," his father cried. "I—I can't believe it."

"Oh!" said the actor. "It's coming out now, is it? I knew there was a conspiracy against me!"

"There's no conspiracy against you," retorted the boy contemptuously. "You killed Mother, and I know it. I know it just as sure as I'm standing here."

"No use of that, son," Smith calmed him. "We're all in for it together, and it won't do much good now to go into that."

"God forgive us, poor miserable sinners!" murmured the Russian.

"You wrong that man," the Count came forward. "He did not kill your mother."

"Of course not," said Smith. "You did. You confessed."

"That confession was a lie," replied the Count calmly.

"Then why did you make it?"

"I had my reasons," he addressed himself to the girl. "I may never have another chance to talk to you, Mary, and I want you to know that in all my life I have never done anything that would make you ashamed of me. Certainly, I could not do so fiendish a thing, so horrible a thing!"

"Then who did kill Mrs. Breese?" demanded Smith. "Not that I care particularly," he amended hastily. "I'm just curious."

"One of us here," replied the Count quietly, "killed Mrs. Breese."

"Name him!" challenged Smith.

"It is not for me to name him," said the Count. "I leave that to his conscience. But I shall tell you what I know. I went to Mrs. Breese's house that night to see you, Mary. Your mother had given strict orders that I was not to be admitted. I made my way in unobserved through the servants' quarters. Then I stole out into the corridor, in the front of the house.

"I saw the front door open and someone come in. That someone opened the door with a key. He went into the drawing-room. I heard voices. Then I saw someone run out, racing into the street. I was puzzled.

"Then Mr. Thomas came down the stairs and went to the drawing-room. He came out quickly and hurried upstairs. Then a moment later the butler came and I heard him cry out that Mrs. Breese had been murdered!"

"The man who preceded Thomas into the drawing-room was the murderer?" said Smith.

"Undoubtedly," replied the Count.

Smith looked about the waiting circle. His eyes rested upon the financier.

"Well, Mr. Breese," he said, smiling grimly, "aren't you ready to tell us yet? After all, what have you got to lose? I can't do a thing to you."

"I?" Breese stammered.

"Yes," said Smith. "You're the man the Count saw walk into that drawing-room. You're the man he's been protecting with his confession."

"You don't think that I killed my wife?" bellowed Breese. "You'd better be careful, young man!"

"What were you doing in your wife's house the night of the murder?" Smith demanded.

"I wasn't there," said Breese. "I don't know what you're talking about."

"Then the Count is lying when he says he saw you there?"

"I told you I wasn't there," snapped the old man.

"You knew your wife was murdered when you talked to me at your hotel," Smith persisted.

"I did not!"

"Strange the vagaries of the human mind!" the Russian suddenly intervened. "Here we are facing death and yet, Mr. Breese, you are as cautious and as canny as if you had something to gain."

"Let me alone!" cried Breese.

"As God is your witness," persisted the Russian, "do you deny that you killed Mrs. Breese?"

"Will you let me alone?" shouted the old man.

"God forgive you," murmured the Russian.

Smith turned to the actor. "How about you, Thomas? The Count says you discovered the body. Is that true? You never told us that!"

"It's true," the actor's voice trembled. "I was afraid to tell you."

"Well, it doesn't matter," said Smith wearily. "Nothing I can do about it."

"I don't want to keep anything back," cried Thomas. "I've gone through hell. I—I lied to you about other things."

"Don't bother," advised Smith. "Let it ride."

"The—the night she was killed," the actor disregarded him, "I didn't tell you—I couldn't—but we quarrelled that night. About—about my wanting to go back. She didn't want me to marry anyone else."

"That's all right," said Smith. "I suppose now that you've gotten that off your mind you'll tell me you short-changed her when she took you out to restaurants."

"No, I didn't," cried the actor. "She always paid herself."

"Quite," said Smith. "Now just to make this a really pleasant party, tell us about the time you played with Mrs. Fiske."

"I—I never played with Mrs. Fiske," protested the actor. "I feel sick. I feel I'm going to faint."

"Not on me," barked Smith, moving away. "Sit down." The actor closed his eyes and sank into a chair. Through the windows a thin jagged line of lightning came to blind us for an instant, and reveal a terrifyingly mountainous sea.

Smith shivered audibly. "I don't know why I'm doing this," he said. "I guess it's habit. I'd like to know one thing from all you—I'd like to know who killed Mrs. Breese. Just my curiosity. There's nothing I can do about it. But I'd like to wind up this case. It's the last one I'll ever handle."

"Why do you assume," demanded Rice angrily, "that any one of us knows who did it?"

"Because," said Smith, "the man who killed Mrs. Breese is sitting right in this room now, looking at me, hoping, waiting, praying, he can keep his secret."

"How do you know he is here?" persisted Rice. "Would he come to the funeral of his victim with us? I think the strain is telling on you, sir."

"I know he's here," replied Smith. "I know it!"

The Russian had risen from his knees. "Mr. Breese!" he cried. "Why don't you tell the truth? Your children are with you. Tell them the truth—if you dare!"

"I've told the truth," muttered Breese.

"You were in that house the night of the murder!" thundered the Russian.

"And supposing I was?" flared Breese.

"Ah!" said the Russian. "You admit you were there!"

"I admit nothing," said Breese. "I'm sick of being badgered. I won't stand for it! Do you hear me? Let me alone!"

The Russian shrugged his shoulders eloquently. He swung on Rice.

"And you, Mr. Rice?"

"What about me?" asked Rice.

"Have you nothing to say?"

"I've been in a lot of tight corners before this," said Rice, "and I've gotten out of them. I see no occasion to entertain you with excerpts from my life."

"Do you know who killed Mrs. Breese?" insisted the Russian.

"If I did," said Rice, "I would take great pleasure in finishing that gentleman off before this boat got me. Now suppose you go back to your prayers and leave us alone."

"You're a poor miserable sinner," cried the Russian. "Sulphur and brimstone await you in hell! You blasphemer!"

"Listen," said Rice, "whatever awaits me, I'll take as my due. I don't need any religion from you. I guess I've done plenty in my life that I'd rather not talk about, but I'll stand the gaff, thank you. Just leave me alone. And if we're passing out, let's pass out like gentlemen, not a bunch of wild hysterical hyenas like you."

"I agree with you," said Smith.

We heard footsteps at the door. Then I saw the Captain walk slowly toward us. He was dripping wet and his eyes were red-rimmed.

Breese jumped up from his chair.

"Well," he cried, "about time you came! What's happened?"

"We've had nasty going," said the Captain. His voice was hoarse. He spoke hardly above a whisper.

"Never mind that," shouted Breese impatiently. "Can you get us out of it?"

"I'm sorry, sir," he reported, "But we've stepped into the path of a cyclone. And I'm afraid we can't weather this storm much longer in our present shape!"

"But you've got to do something!" cried Breese.

"There's nothing to do, sir," replied the Captain quietly. "We're in a rather bad way!"

"Do you mean to tell me," cried Breese, "that you're standing by with folded hands and letting us go to our deaths? Man, are you mad?"

The Captain turned on his heel wearily and left Breese expostulating to thin air. The Russian had fallen to his knees.

"God forgive them, miserable sinners," he shouted above the howling of the wind. "Forgive the miserable sinner, Thomas, who lied and cheated from his cradle. He did not know what he was doing. Forgive the arrogant Breese.

Forgive the unbeliever, Rice. Forgive the children. Forgive us all, as we come to you from the bottom of the sea!"

Strange cries mingled with the prayer. We ran to the door, trying to peer into the black darkness. The yacht tossed, and hurled us violently at each other, and against the walls.

The Russian prayed on.

Then I saw our radio man moving toward Perutkin. I had paid no attention to him heretofore. He seemed oddly out of place among these people—a colorless, humdrum, frightened little fellow.

He sank to his knees beside the Russian and he tapped the giant's shoulder.

"What is it, my son?" Perutkin halted his prayer and looked gently at the mechanic.

"Will you—pray for me?" he begged.

"Certainly, my son," replied the Russian. "I shall pray for you."

"I've—I've got something on my mind," the operator groaned inarticulately. "I've—I've got something to tell you."

Even then, when I was concerned with my own fate, I wondered what the little man could be keeping from the world in his narrow bosom. Something trivial, I knew, that would appear ludicrous in the light of the impending tragedy.

But Breese had come over to us. He looked down upon the two kneeling figures with contemptuous wrath.

"Praying!" he shouted. "Why don't you go to work—get that wireless going? Damn cowards!"

"Yes, you two! Great revival meeting you're putting on," Rice chimed in. "It makes me sick to look at you!"

"Don't listen to them," counselled the Russian. "Pray, my son."

"Get up!" shouted Breese hysterically. "Stop it, I tell you!"

"I won't," cried the mechanic. "I won't. I got something to tell. I got something on my mind. I'm going to tell. You can't stop me. I've been listening to all of you. I didn't know—" he gasped for breath. "I thought—about Mrs. Breese—I——"

"What about Mrs. Breese?" Smith asked quietly.

"I—I—don't look at me like that—I—" He moaned as if in pain.

Suddenly the flash-light upon the table was hurled to the floor. We were plunged in darkness.

"Go on," cried the Russian. "Quick—what about Mrs. Breese? Who killed her?"

"Wait, can't you?" the mechanic cried. "I'll tell you! I'll tell you——"

A revolver shot boomed in my ear. I heard the man groan. I heard his body fall to the floor.

Suddenly, miraculously, the lights flared up in the room and through the ship!

The Russian was kneeling over the prone figure. He raised his head, and his sharp little eyes travelled over the room.

"He's dead," said the Russian slowly.

CHAPTER XIX
THE MURDER ON THE YACHT

BEFORE ANY OF US could move, before we could realize what had happened, the stilled engines of the yacht were throbbing once more, and we were ploughing ahead. The storm still raged, but now our craft cut the waters with disdain.

But no one moved for a moment. We were all staring in grim fascination at the absurd figure of the humdrum little operator upon the floor. He seemed so unreal there.

Breese was the first to cry out to the rest of us the inexplicable fact that our craft had suddenly taken on life. Then, as I recall the hectic moments, Rice ran to the window, as if he did not believe his senses. Others followed him—that is, the elder Breese did, and the actor. The Countess still stood as if in a dream. The Count maintained his solitary position in the corner. All our movements, now that I try to reconstruct them, had the unearthly quality of a dream.

Then I heard the actor call: "We're saved! Hang it all, we're saved!" He slobbered in his relief. Tears streaked his cheeks.

The Countess cried out, as if she were waking. Then I realized the Count was at her side. She was in his arms, and laughing and crying in turn in her hysteria.

"Take her to her cabin," Perutkin ordered. "The rest of you stay here."

"But what's happened?" demanded Breese. He seemed utterly bewildered.

"Perhaps you've already guessed," countered the Russian strangely. "A man has been murdered."

"Never mind that!" Breese's contempt for the figure before us chilled me. "What's happened with the ship? We're moving."

The Russian did not reply. The Countess was now sobbing as her former husband led her from the room.

"You will be good enough to return immediately," Perutkin called after his protégé, who nodded. Then to the rest of us: "None of you will leave this room."

"Are we still in danger or not? That's what I want to know!" Breese cried, straining to look out of the window.

"One of us is out of danger," the Russian said slowly, pointing to the figure.

The Captain emerged from the corridor. He stopped short at the sight of the body of his operator.

"How did this happen?" he demanded sharply. The Russian shrugged his shoulders. The Captain's thin lips set in one hard line. "You're responsible for this," he said sternly.

"But it was not in my plan!" protested the Russian. "How could I know such a disaster was possible?"

"What plan?" demanded Breese, listening open-mouthed, as we all did, to the puzzling dialogue.

"You must know, Mr. Breese!" replied the Russian. "Surely you must have guessed by now."

"You're talking in riddles," snapped Breese. "What is it?"

The Captain addressed his employer. "Sir, you have every right to discharge me," he began. "At no time during this trip were we in any danger. This man—" pointing to Perutkin—"asked me to convince you that the ship was going down. He said I would help trap the murderer of Mrs. Breese."

"Certainly," added the Russian. "It was a feasible plan. I argued that the murderer of Mrs. Breese must be on this yacht. I argued that if we could convince him that he faced death, he might be trapped into a confession. He would feel he had nothing to lose. Unfortunately—" the Russian gestured helplessly and it was not necessary for him to conclude.

"You mean—you deliberately—staged this—this hoax!" Breese sputtered.

"Yes," replied the Captain, "every bit of it. We did damage the wireless set, but there was nothing else wrong. And it cost one poor fellow his life."

"Because," explained the Russian, "the murderer was clever enough, Mr. Breese, to guess our plan. I am amazed that a man like you was fooled." Once more his sharp little eyes stared at Breese. Then he continued smoothly: "It was all in very bad taste, I'll grant you. I could not resist the temptation of the storm. It seemed a sign from the heavens."

"We're wasting time," intervened Smith. "I want to ask you, Captain, what you know of this poor chap?"

"His name is Louis Trenholm," replied the Captain methodically. "I think he was thirty-one. If I remember rightly I signed him on myself—he came from Olean, New York. I don't remember that he had any living relatives."

Smith noted these sparse details in his note-book.

"How long had he been with you?" asked Smith.

"Just about a week," replied the Captain. "Our regular man—Wilkins—resigned when we got to Havana to go with the Dollar Line. Wilkins recommended this man and I signed him on. That's all I know about him."

"Very good, Captain," approved Perutkin. "You tell us much. For if this man was signed on after the yacht arrived in Havana he never met Mrs. Breese to your knowledge, did he?"

"I don't follow," said the Captain, puzzled.

"Why, it's simple enough," said the Russian. "You told us that you signed him on *after* Mrs. Breese left the yacht. So that as far as you know they had never met."

"Yes, that's true," said the Captain.

"And yet," continued the Russian, "this man knew who killed Mrs. Breese!"

"I won't hear any more of it," the elder Breese suddenly shouted. "You can't stand around here and talk of things that mean so much to my family and me!" He trembled violently. He seemed on the verge of collapse. "Get this ship into port just as fast as you can. Don't stand there!" This at the Captain, who turned on his heel abruptly and left without a word.

"But one moment!" interposed the Russian. "I am astounded, Mr. Breese. I sympathize with your feelings, but you still don't seem to realize that a murderer may be standing not more than four feet away from you at this very moment. Don't you want that murderer punished?"

"Certainly! But you're punishing my family, not the murderer, with all this—this—tomfoolery!" cried Breese. "I'm going down to my cabin, and I don't want to hear anything about it. It's up to you to arrest the man who is responsible, and when you've done that I'll be very glad to hear it." Leaning on the arm of his son, he made for the door.

"Let him go," advised Rice. "The strain has been too much for him. He doesn't realize what's happened."

"Exactly," said the Russian. "I trust he may later. Now to you gentlemen who remain I must explain that our situation here is rather unique. Let me put it as clearly as I can. Mr. Smith and I believed that we could fool all of you into a state where you would fancy yourselves facing death. We had reason to suppose that the murderer of Mrs. Breese was on this yacht.

"We expected the murderer to crack, to confess. But the only man who broke down was this poor fellow here. Obviously he was not the murderer of Mrs. Breese. As far as we can learn, he did not even know her. Therefore, we are led to assume the conclusion that the real murderer was not convinced by our hoax.

"And—he was so sufficiently sure of himself that he took this opportunity of getting rid of the one man who knew something of the murder. What that something is no one can even guess." He paused for breath. Then he smiled quizzically, as he looked about him. "One of us here, on this yacht, killed this man. Either you, my friend," to the Count who had returned just then and was standing in the doorway, "either you, Mr. Thomas, either you, Mr. Rice, or the three members of the Breese family who have left us."

"Well, I had nothing to do with it," cried the actor. "Hang it all, you're not going to begin all over again with me."

"No," said the Russian. "You see, we are in a much better position than we were before. In a crime committed in a house, people may go and come unseen. But we know all those who are on this boat. Our search narrows down considerably. For example, our first step is to locate the revolver with which this murder was committed. Have any of you gentlemen a revolver?"

"Not me!" cried the actor. "Why should I have a revolver?"

"I did not address you alone," said the Russian. "I assume that none of you gentlemen will produce a revolver for me. It is too much to expect." He smiled. "Shall we search them, Mr. Smith?"

"I don't think that'll be necessary," said Smith. He put his hand in his pocket and produced a pearl-handled weapon. He clicked open the barrel. "There's been one shot fired—this is undoubtedly the gun that was used."

"Where did you find it?" demanded the Russian.

"In my pocket," said Smith. "It also happens to be my gun."

CHAPTER XX
THE LETTER

"YOURS?" EXCLAIMED RICE, STARING at the detective.

"Yes," said Smith. "The man who murdered Trenholm took this gun out of my pocket, fired one shot, and put it back into my pocket immediately afterwards."

"But how clever!" admired the Russian. Smith flushed.

"I don't know how clever he is," he muttered. "It was dark and the boat was pitching."

"But you felt nothing?" demanded the Russian.

"Nothing at all," replied Smith.

"According to your own formula," the Russian's eyes twinkled, "you are the guilty person, Mr. Smith. All the evidence is on your person."

"I don't think this is a joke," Smith looked at him cuttingly.

"But it is not without its humor," insisted the Russian. "Don't you think so, Mr. Thomas?" He swung at the actor.

"Damned funny!" giggled the actor.

"Beyond me," commented Rice. "Can't think—I'm dizzy!"

Smith finally dismissed the three men. When the door closed upon them, he blazed at the Russian: "Fine idea you sold me! We're in deeper than ever now."

"No!" protested the Russian. "We are one step ahead."

"Theoretically, yes," said Smith. "Theoretically we know that someone in this room with us killed Trenholm because he was going to spill. Theoretically we can hammer away at everyone until we get the right man. Actually, we can do nothing of the kind. We can't hold the Breese family. I'd lose my job. Breese is a pretty important man. We'll have to let them all go until we get evidence. And the only evidence we have is this revolver. I'll get our finger-print man to see what he can find."

"I'll grant you all that," replied the Russian. "Our problem is not easy. I shall go further. The man who did this murder wouldn't be fool enough to leave finger-prints. I attach no importance to that. It was a simple matter for him to wipe the revolver clean before he put it back. It takes but an instant to pass a handkerchief over a revolver."

"Then what am I going to do?" demanded Smith. "I'm going to look fine when I make my report. Right under my nose another murder is pulled off! Won't that look marvellous—for me!"

"Well," said the Russian, pacing up and down, "there are several things we can do. Let me see—I was kneeling here, the operator beside me." He went about the room indicating the position of each occupant. "Now the bullet entered this man's heart. It came from this direction. Who was sitting here? Well—we have first, Mr. Breese, his son, and his daughter. Rice was not far away. The Count was in back of them. Any one of them could have killed this man."

"That's not much help," said Smith. "The man who did it did considerable moving in the dark. He must have, to have gotten my gun and put it back again."

"But let us forget the physical aspects of the case," continued the Russian. "Let us inquire further into motive. We know that Trenholm knew who killed Mrs. Breese. Now the question is—how did he know? Apparently he had never met Mrs. Breese. Apparently he had never been to her home. Had he perhaps overheard some vital information while he was on this boat? But his manner was not that. His manner was such that in some way he was vitally implicated in the murder of Mrs. Breese. How, I cannot tell you."

"But that doesn't get us anywhere," Smith snorted. "You can stand here and theorize from morning to night. The fact is we've got no evidence. The first thing I want to do is to search his effects."

"Very well," said the Russian. "Begin with his clothes."

With professional briskness, the two began the ghastly job of dragging forth the contents of the man's pockets. A cheap watch with the picture of an adenoidal girl in its case—a pocket knife, two Yale keys, a tattered New York automobile license, a clipping of a poem by Eddie Guest, a wallet. Smith expertly turned it inside out. It was a cheap wallet, the kind usually accompanied by the yellow printed card: "My name—height—weight— In case of accident, notify— The size of my collar is—" He had laboriously filled out the card. The Y. M. C. A. of Olean was to be notified of accident. From the folds of the wallet Smith dragged forward a letter. He looked at it hastily, and then held it in his hand. He turned to the Russian. "Look at this!" he invited.

"Dear Louis," the handwriting was stiff and angular, obviously written by an illiterate man. "I been thinking it over, and I think you're a darn fool. We can clean up if you let me handle it. Why don't you come and see me like you use to. Yours, Charlie."

"No return address," Smith said, examining the envelope. "Mailed in Havana. We might trace it."

"But who is Charlie?" demanded the Russian. "It may or may not be relevant—this letter. Perhaps our friend had an invention. You remember the man was a mechanic. Charlie is advising him to capitalize it in characteristic American fashion."

"No," said Smith, "this letter smells blackmail to me. I've handled enough of those cases to know."

"Yes," conceded the Russian. "I see. Trenholm knew who killed Mrs. Breese and told Charlie. Charlie said 'Get money.' Quite likely. That is a feasible interpretation. I admit I did not think of it, Mr. Smith. It's decidedly worth looking into."

They pawed over a few trinkets and odds and ends and then decided that their task was done.

"We'll go down to his berth and look into that," said Smith. "Can't tell what we may stumble on. He may have other letters from Charlie."

We rang for the steward, who guided us to the narrow cabin that the operator shared with the third mate. The latter was sound asleep when we entered. He rubbed his eyes as Smith explained our purpose.

"Damn shame," he said, indicating the battered trunk under the berth that had been occupied by Trenholm. "Nice quiet chap, he was. How did it happen?"

Smith was uncommunicative. He bent down to open the trunk. It was locked.

"Give me a knife!" begged the Russian. "I have a knack with these objects." Smith gave him a pen-knife and in a few moments the Russian threw the lid back. The trunk was empty.

"That's funny," muttered the young officer. "He always had his trunk crammed with stuff—plans, tools, all kinds of junk. I remember kidding him about it. He had a lot of blue prints."

"When did you last see this trunk open?" asked Smith. The young man stopped to think. "Wait a minute," he said suddenly. "Just this evening! I almost forgot. Trenholm came in here as I was turning in. He was putting something away."

"And the trunk was full?"

"Oh yes." Then he volunteered: "He was a peculiar chap, you know."

"In what way?" demanded Smith.

"Well, in a general way," the young officer replied vaguely. "Of course, I didn't know much about him. He's only been with us a week, and you don't generally get to know much about a chap in a week. He kept to himself more or less, if you know what I mean. He wasn't very talkative."

"Was he working upon any inventions that you know of?" asked the Russian.

"I think he was," said the officer. "Most radio men do. But I don't know definitely that he was."

"Perhaps you could tell us if he ever talked of any friends in Havana."

"No, but he must have had some friends. He signed on here."

"One more question," said the Russian. "To your knowledge, did Trenholm know any of the passengers on this yacht?"

The officer shook his head. "I hardly think so. We've had no passengers since he signed on—until tonight."

In the corridor, the Russian said: "Behold! The man we want not only takes your revolver and shoots Trenholm, but after the murder comes down here and removes the dead man's effects."

"I got that," said Smith.

"Now!" said the Russian. "Think back. We have six suspects—Mr. Breese, his son, his daughter, Mr. Thomas and Mr. Rice and the Count. Put yourself in the murderer's place. Having committed his crime, he will be very anxious to steal down below and get at Trenholm's effects. Follow the course of action——"

"The Countess goes into hysterics," began Smith.

"And the Count takes her out," I added.

"At my suggestion," corrected the Russian, "and he returns almost immediately. Behold! I deliberately order everyone else to remain. I cleverly foresaw that the murderer would have further work to do, and would be anxious to leave the room. Now, who made a move to go? Thomas? No. Rice? No."

"That leaves Breese," said Smith.

"That leaves Breese," repeated the Russian. "He, and he alone, insisted upon leaving the room. Why?"

No one answered him. I realized that the engines had stopped once more. Through the windows I could make out the shadowy outlines of the port and, far-off, twinkling lights.

"We're coming in," I cried in relief.

"It is a symbol, my friends," the Russian said, rubbing his hands. "Our experiment has not been such a failure. We have reached the end of our journey. At last we know our man. Tomorrow we shall have him!"

CHAPTER XXI
THE RAID

MY TELEPHONE RANG PERSISTENTLY. I had just waked out of a sleep of exhaustion and reached for it with sleep-numbed fingers.

"Perutkin speaking!" the voice boomed. "Meet me in the lobby of the Biltmore in twenty minutes!" The words were a command. My wishes were not consulted. But I agreed readily enough. Most people did when Perutkin commanded.

So I dressed hastily and gulped my weak coffee. A cab deposited me at the Biltmore a few moments before the appointed time. I saw no sign of the Russian and made myself comfortable with a week-old New York newspaper and a cigar.

Several moments later the bulk of the Russian loomed over me. "Put away that paper," he whispered. "I shall give you something more appetizing than an editor's fancies. Rise from your chair and nonchalantly as you can follow me to the elevator."

"Why? What?" I demanded.

"Ask nothing. And do not look so surprised. We are going upstairs."

As he said this, he preceded me into the elevator cage.

"Seventh," he barked at the boy. And then to me: "Well, are you enjoying yourself? A most interesting city, is it not? Or do you confine your wanderings to Sloppy Joe's, like all Americans?"

I mumbled something. But by this time we had alighted. He strode forward confidently. Then I realized that we were approaching the suite of Henry Breese.

"We're not going to see the old man?" I demanded.

"Quiet!" whispered the Russian, as a bell boy whisked past us. "We are not going to see anyone." He stopped in front of Breese's door. He reached into his pocket and extracted a miniature jimmy. This he inserted in the lock and the door opened almost instantly. He dragged me into the room—I could not move—and then closed the door behind him.

"We are doing a little burglary," he explained casually. "I needed a companion in crime and I chose you. Are you not flattered?"

"But what are you going to do—and why?" I insisted.

"It's simple enough," he said carelessly. "I'm going to search Mr. Breese's room very thoroughly. That is all. If you are afraid we shall be interrupted, let me inform you that Mr. Breese will be occupied for several hours. I have ascertained that. The chambermaid has already made the beds and issued the towels. We are quite safe. You see, I am a good burglar. I know what I'm at. Any detective worthy of the name who cannot be a better burglar than the regular members of the profession really has no reason for existence."

"But do you think," I demanded, "that Breese would leave anything in his room calculated to arouse our suspicions?"

"Why not?" demanded the Russian, proceeding to the secretary, and opening a drawer. While he was examining papers he said: "You must understand this about crimes and criminals: At a certain stage every criminal is exact, methodical and cunning. Then he becomes desperate and may do something brilliant—such as the killing of Trenholm with Smith's own pistol. Our friend Smith has not yet recovered from his chagrin at that. In fact, it hurts more now than ever. But as the pace becomes more furious for the criminal he becomes careless. He must relax. He must overlook something." He put back carefully letters, telegrams. "And we may find something. I do not guarantee it. But I am hoping."

I called out suddenly, for I heard soft footfalls approaching outside. The Russian paused, listening. Then the door next to ours opened and I breathed more easily.

"There is only one thing," the Russian said. "I have not devised a means of exit if we are surprised. I do not expect to be surprised. But if the worst comes to the worst, Mr. Smith can always rescue us from the law. A trifle! In my own country I have consistently broken all laws."

He was now at the wardrobe closet, expertly fumbling into the pockets of Mr. Breese's carefully tailored suits.

"But the man is rich!" he exclaimed. "Such textiles! Such cloth! I have always bought the best when I could afford it, and I flatter myself my taste in clothes is superior to any man's. Unfortunately, at the moment I cannot indulge it. I always had my clothes made in England when I was in my glory," he sighed. "However—what have we here?" He held up a piece of brown wrapping paper. I thought it strange that Breese should carry such an obviously dirty piece of paper on his person. "Look!" cried the Russian.

Peering over his shoulder, I saw that these words had been scrawled upon the paper:

"Dear Mr. Breese," I read. "Please come and see me right away as I have important info. and it will pay you. Don't fail to come as this is *important*. I will be waiting for you tonight at 7 in my shop 32 Calle C and 3rd Street. Charles Spence."

"Charles Spence!" exclaimed the Russian. "I wonder if it can be the Charlie who advised Trenholm on just such paper and in just such writing to get money!"

"It must be," I exclaimed.

"Smith has that letter," the Russian continued. "If we could compare, we could make sure. But obviously it must be the same man. And we have his address—Calle C and 3rd Street." He put the paper carefully back into the pocket he had just rifled. "We shall proceed there immediately. Come!"

When the Russian moved, he moved quickly. I found myself panting after him as he strode down the corridor. We waited for the elevator. Just as we were about to get in, the elder Breese emerged.

He frowned on us, and did not even nod. For his part, the Russian ignored him and stepped into the elevator cage.

Down in the lobby, he said: "Unless I miss my guess, Mr. Breese has forgotten that note. He is wearing a suit not unlike the one I examined. He probably was on his way to see our Charlie and then discovered he had forgotten the address. We shall wait."

We waited in easy chairs screened by pillars so the elder Breese did not see us when he emerged once more and hurried out. The Russian beckoned to me and we followed slowly. When we reached the street, Breese was already in a cab. The Russian permitted him to disappear around a corner before he summoned a cab for us and directed our driver to take us to Calle C and 3rd.

"A highly interesting man, Breese," the Russian lectured on our way down. "If my theories are right—and I have no reason to doubt them—he will probably go down in history as one of the world's most interesting criminals. And why not? When a respectable and cultivated man goes in for crime he makes the efforts of the professionals look childish in comparison. Most criminals are merely mental deficients.

"What I admire in him is his attitude toward us. Most criminals would be bland, friendly. They would be very careful not to antagonize the police. With what result? The clever detective sees through them. Not so with Breese. He takes pains to antagonize us. Why? Because, he reasons, we will assume he has nothing to fear. He is merely standing on his rights."

"But is his attitude so unnatural?" I asked. "After all, he's an arrogant man."

"He was not arrogant when he warned Smith of his wife's danger an hour after she was murdered. He was polite enough when he tried to explain away his possession of a key to the Gilded Cage. There are moments when he shows fear. But he is a man of considerable strength of mind. After all, he reasons he can leave for the States at any moment now. Then he is safe. The case will be forgotten. He is not in a bad position, Mr. Breese. In fact, he is in a very good position. I do not boast, but his sole misfortune is that I happen to be interested in the case. Other criminals have discovered that before him!"

He leaned back contentedly and let the sun warm his ruddy face. We were passing through Havana's slum section. Colored urchins as naked as the day they were born rolled in the sand. Black women were grouped in front of flimsy shacks in the community kitchen, for the primitive cooking on charcoal fires was done in the open. Every so often a butcher's cart full of live chickens, guinea hens and peacocks rolled by under the guidance of a somnolent coolie.

About a block from our destination, we dismissed the cab and walked past a series of open stores and shabby brick homes. We spied a small sign: "Charles Spence—Bicycles—Repairs."

In front of the shop, a taxi waited. I recognized it as the one Breese had engaged. The Russian stopped a few feet away from the store.

"We shall wait here," he said.

"Well, I'll wait for you!" The Russian swung around. I started. Smith was at my elbow.

"Where did you come from?" the Russian chuckled. "But you are bright this morning, Mr. Smith!"

"I was just about going to ask you the same question," Smith smiled jovially. He seemed unusually buoyant. There was an air of triumph about him.

The Russian explained how we found the note. Smith grinned.

"You went to a lot of unnecessary trouble," he said somewhat patronizingly to the Russian. "It so happens that this morning I got a letter from Mr. Spence asking me to call."

"And then you saw Mr. Breese walk in?" concluded the Russian.

"No, I called first and after I had gone out I saw Mr. Breese walk in." He shook his head reflectively. "Very funny chap, Spence. I had a long talk with him."

"Well, I am listening!" the Russian boomed. "Tell me!"

"Well," drawled Smith, "I'll tell you exactly what happened. I got a letter saying this: 'Call at Calle C and 3rd—Charles Spence.' I discovered that Mr. Spence was a rather gangly chap, with very sharp eyes. If I'm not mistaken, it's T. B. with him, and he came down originally for the climate. Well, he hemmed and hawed a lot before he got started, and then hemmed and hawed a lot more when he did. What it all came down to was this: he wanted to know how much there was in it for him if he told all he knew about the Breese murder. I had to tell him there was no reward, but that I'd see to it that he was well paid. In fact, I said I'd be willing to give a year's salary myself just to clear the case. He hemmed and hawed some more."

"But didn't he give you any inkling of what he knew?" interrupted the Russian.

"He made it pretty plain," replied Smith, "that he got his information from Trenholm."

"Who had never met Mrs. Breese," said the Russian.

"Yes, I put that up to him," replied Smith. "But he only smiled a kind of wet smile and let it go at that. He said he knew and he had the evidence and it was just a question of whether I would pay. Well, naturally, I got excited. I tried to pin him down. When he wouldn't come across, I threatened to arrest him as a material witness. He got frightened at that. I guess he had forgotten to figure on that. But he was pretty obstinate. Well, finally I said I'd give him an hour to think it over. I left, and just as I got down here I saw Breese's cab draw up."

"Hmm," the Russian reflected. "You have handled matters very badly, Mr. Smith."

"How do you get that?" Smith demanded resentfully.

"It is quite obvious," replied the Russian. "The man is greedy. He has a piece of information implicating Breese. He knows that Breese is obstinate. He is obviously blackmailing him. He thinks that perhaps, if Breese fails to pay, then the police will give him something substantial. You should have promised him at least fifty thousand dollars. It costs nothing to promise."

"I don't have to promise him anything," countered Smith. "I can lock him up any time and he'll come through all right. I'm not worried about him. This case is over. What with Breese coming down and Charlie Spence handy where I can get him I expect to have something in a very short time."

"Which leads me to the conclusion," said the Russian, "that all my bright hopes have been shattered. I'm going to see Mr. Spence myself."

"Not while Breese is in there!" exclaimed Smith.

"But why not? I want Breese to know that I am here. It will help matters considerably. Come!"

I knew the Russian well enough by this time to know that he would be in Charles Spence's bicycle store within a moment and I plunged after him.

Mr. Spence's window contained one highly polished wire-wheeled bicycle, a collection of patched tires and an incongruous monkey wrench. The window had not been washed in many years. It is something of an eccentricity to have a shop window in Havana. The natives use shutters.

As we entered the dark store I was surprised to find no one in sight. The Russian knocked loudly upon a small work-table. Still no one answered.

"As I feared," he muttered. "Mr. Smith should be spanked."

"There must be someone here," I ventured. "Breese's cab is still outside."

"We shall try the door," the Russian decided, pointing to the little door leading obviously to another work shop. He thrust this open. The elder Breese, who had been sitting at a table, sprang up.

"Greetings, Mr. Breese," boomed the Russian. The old man said nothing. "We should like to see your friend, Charlie Spence." Still the old man did not answer. "Surely you will be good enough to tell us where we can find him, no?"

"I'm waiting for him myself," the old man said finally, glaring at the Russian.

"Then we shall wait, too," said the Russian. He seated himself directly opposite the financier, and leaned over toward him. "That is what I admire in you Americans—your great democracy. Who would think that so important a man as you would have so humble a friend as Spence? It is remarkable!"

Breese grunted.

"Did you say something, Mr. Breese?" demanded the Russian.

"No, I didn't," snapped Breese.

The Russian bowed with mock courtesy. "I don't expect you to talk to me. But it's really no use, Mr. Breese. No use at all. This man Spence wants your money—and yet what good will it do you? We have the evidence. Believe me, Mr. Breese, he is merely making a fool of you."

"What in the world are you talking about?" sputtered the financier.

"Surely my meaning is quite plain," retorted the Russian. "You received a letter from Mr. Spence this morning. Mr. Spence is—or rather, was—a friend of our wireless operator who was killed so mysteriously. Mr. Spence has the same information that caused that poor fellow's death. Only Mr. Spence does not intend to suffer the same fate. He intends to enrich himself and at your expense. Well, Mr. Breese, are you ready to talk now?"

"About what?" snapped Breese. "I got a letter the other day from this man and a very strange telephone call. He said he had some information on my wife's death. I came here this morning. I met him. He asked me to wait. He said he had business a few doors away. I've been waiting for him ever since."

"Almost plausible!" said the Russian.

"Damn it, do you think I'm lying to you?" shouted Breese.

"I know you are," replied the Russian coolly. "Be good enough to tell us where Mr. Spence is. What have you done with him?"

"What have I done with him? Man, are you mad?" Breese sputtered feebly. "I've got a good mind to report you to your superiors."

"Here is my superior now," the Russian called, as Smith swung the door open. Smith's face was grave. The Russian sensed that something had happened.

"What's wrong?" he demanded. "Have you found Spence?"

"No," said Smith. "But Mr. Spence just drove away post-haste in your cab, Mr. Breese. And when I called to him he seemed very anxious not to hear."

"I can't understand it," muttered Breese.

"I can," said the Russian. "Mr. Spence's plans went slightly wrong. Mr. Smith threatened him with arrest. And you, Mr. Breese, threatened him with his life. Caught between the devil and the deep sea, he ran away."

"You think that I—I threatened him?"

"Certainly."

"You must be mad! You must be!"

"There's an easy way of testing that," challenged the Russian. "For example, if it should so happen that you carry a weapon at this moment, no jury would declare me mad for believing that you threatened your humble friend. Do you carry a revolver?"

"I do carry a revolver," Breese conceded hesitantly, after an uncomfortable pause.

"Ah!" exclaimed the Russian.

"I didn't know where I was going. I took it along for protection."

"May I have that revolver?" Smith asked, extending his hand. Reluctantly the old man surrendered the weapon.

"Thank you," said Smith. "Now, Mr. Breese, I think you should know that I've gotten Spence's full story," Smith lied easily. "I was here before you came—and—there's no use holding it back from you—he told me enough to warrant your arrest. I'm afraid I'll have to ask you to go down to Headquarters with me."

"Arrest me—for what?" shouted the old man.

"For the murder of your wife and the murder of Louis Trenholm."

The old man looked from Smith to the Russian, and then at me.

"I suppose you're all quite sane," he said finally. "I may be mad myself. I shouldn't wonder, with all I've been through. But just what is the reason for my arrest?" He was quite calm now, as if striving hard to maintain his composure in a bewildering situation.

"I'm afraid I can't tell you," the Russian shook his head. "As far as I know there is not a single piece of evidence against you." I could not believe my ears. Smith could only stare.

"Look here——" bellowed Smith.

The Russian held up his hand.

"Not a word, Mr. Smith. I've led you astray. This is not our man. We've been fools—utter fools!" Then he muttered, "Bicycles! Wireless operator! Don't you see?" He paced up and down excitedly. "It is incredible that I missed it. Utterly incredible. I am ashamed! I am senile!" Then suddenly he shouted: "Come—come before it is too late! Follow me!"

He bounded out of the room.

CHAPTER XXII
THE MAN IN THE TAXI

"WOULD YOU MIND TELLING me—" the elder Breese was exasperatingly polite—"if your police department is composed solely of lunatics?"

Smith swallowed helplessly. I could sympathize with his exasperation. The Russian had persistently hammered at him to arrest Breese. When Smith finally in desperation had taken this step the irrepressible Perutkin sent his own house of cards toppling, and was off.

But the detective stuck to his guns. "You needn't pay any attention to him," he said. "He'll have nothing more to do with this case. I'll see to that. I'm in charge and I'll take full responsibility, Mr. Breese, for whatever I do."

"Very well, then," said Breese. "Am I to understand that I am under arrest for murder?"

"Exactly," snapped Smith.

"I suppose I'm permitted to consult a lawyer?" the old man asked coolly.

"In due time," replied Smith. "You needn't answer any questions I put to you but if you really know nothing of the murder of your wife and of Trenholm, being frank with me will save a lot of unpleasantness."

Breese nodded. "This is not unexpected," he confessed. "I've caught you people looking strangely at me and it's gotten on my nerves. Now what evidence will you present in court?"

"First," said Smith, "you had a key which gave you entrance to your wife's house."

"That's a long way from murder," said the old man.

"You used that key that night."

"And if I did?"

"You knew your wife was dead when we came to your room that night. When you got the news over the telephone, you acted as if it were news to you. You did your utmost to implicate Thomas."

"Because I sincerely believed him to be at the bottom of it, and I'm not sure now that I've changed my mind."

"But a man of your standing," insisted Smith, "doesn't usually play hide and seek with the police the way you did unless he has something to hide."

"I've got some imagination," replied Breese. "My relations with my wife were not of the best. In the eyes of the law I had plenty of motive to kill her. But the law doesn't realize that a man who loves a woman doesn't kill her no matter how much she exasperates him. But I knew that if it were known that I was in the house at the time—that I had, in fact, stolen into the house—you people would make short work of me. I had to protect myself."

"That sounds reasonable, the way you tell it," conceded Smith.

"It's the truth," the old man said simply. "Good God, man, do I look like a murderer? Do I look like a man who would kill the woman who bore me two children?"

"But here's the problem we're up against," Smith pointed out. "We've got to proceed on evidence. Slowly but surely the evidence has been accumulating against you. You admit it yourself. If you didn't kill her, who did?"

"Do you think that if I knew I wouldn't have told you long ago?" countered the old man. "Don't you think I loved my wife? Don't you think her death was a blow to me? Don't you think I'm suffering the torments of hell right now?"

There was such evident sincerity in the man's voice that even Smith, I could see, was troubled. He said: "I want you to understand, Mr. Breese, that I'm merely doing my duty." The old man nodded. "But there are still actions of yours that I can't explain away. Why were you so anxious to leave the country before your wife's funeral? I had to go to the trouble of getting you shipped back from Key West."

"Oh, you were the one?" the old man smiled grimly. "I suspected as much. Well, I did want to get away. You remember you told me that the Count had been arrested on his confession. I know how my daughter feels about him. Coming at that time, I felt I had all the sorrow I could bear. I wanted to get away to think things out. I was afraid of breaking under the strain." He paused. "As a matter of fact, I consulted Rice and asked his advice. He advised me to go away. He knew I had nothing to do with it and he was perfectly willing to look after my family."

"You should have consulted me," Smith said. "If you'd talked as frankly as you do now we'd have been much further ahead in this case."

"I had no desire to tangle myself up with the police," the old man pointed out.

"Well, then, finally," said Smith, "just why did you come to see Mr. Spence?"

"If a man writes me to come and see him, and then telephones me he has information on my wife's death, I'd naturally come. As a matter of fact, I paid no attention to the letter, because it was so cryptic. It was only after he phoned me that I decided to look into the matter."

"Why didn't you refer Spence to me?" demanded Smith.

"I'm in the habit of doing things for myself," replied Breese. "I wasn't afraid to come down. I took a revolver along as a precaution. I had no real reason to be afraid. And perhaps you're willing to believe that I'm just as anxious to clear up my wife's death as anyone can be. I feel I'm under a shadow until the case is cleared."

From Smith's bland expression I knew that he was studying the financier with great interest. I knew that Smith had not yet made up his mind.

"You must understand," Smith continued, "that your visit here, coupled with other circumstances, is highly suspicious. Let me show you why—I talked with Spence. He's a blackmailer. He wants money. Any jury would assume that he wrote you for only one purpose—to get hush money. And that you came down to give it to him."

"But I never heard of the man before!" cried Breese.

"But you heard of Trenholm."

"No," said Breese. "I didn't. First I saw of him was the night of the funeral, although I was paying him his salary. That Trenholm business is absolutely beyond me. That whole night is like a nightmare to me even now. I woke up last night shivering and sweating. I'd been dreaming all sorts of crazy things, with Trenholm in them. It's taken all my will power, I tell you, to keep my hold on things."

Smith looked at him. For my part, I was willing to accept the financier's story. I had realized before that a chain of circumstantial evidence may strangle the innocent, and Breese seemed to have a tenable explanation for every step he took in the case, once you granted him a lack of motive. On the other hand, I realized (and Smith, I could see, was of the same mind) that Breese might be wriggling out of the evidence against him with a disarming frankness foreign to his character.

Finally Smith said: "I'm willing to go a long way, Mr. Breese, to give you the benefit of the doubt—provided you promise me that you won't leave the country until I say you can go."

Something of the financier's arrogance returned to him. He flushed angrily. "And what if I refuse?"

Smith shrugged his shoulders. "Then I'm afraid I must take the necessary steps to detain you."

He spoke quietly, but there was a challenge in his voice. The old man stared at him defiantly.

But the tension was broken by the door swinging open suddenly. A young native in the livery of a taxi chauffeur stood panting before us. I recognized him as Breese's driver. His eyes were wide open with excitement, and his forehead was wet.

"Mr. Breese!" he called. "Mr. Breese!"

"What is it?" growled the financier.

"Come with me, please. Right away!" the driver pleaded. "There's a man in the cab."

"What man?" demanded Breese.

"The man you sent away with me."

"I didn't send any man away with you," Breese denied angrily. "What are you talking about?"

But the chauffeur was now wringing his hands. "Come please!" he pleaded. "It is terrible."

"What's come over you?" demanded Breese.

"Come—please—see" urged the chauffeur, wringing his hands more violently. "It is terrible!" Then he stopped, realizing our utter bewilderment. He began patiently. "I am sitting outside, waiting for you, Mr. Breese, when a man runs out from back of the store and he says: 'Mr. Breese want you to drive me quick to Calle L.' So I says: 'Get in.' So we drive."

"I didn't send anyone to you," Breese shook his head. "I haven't met anyone here except Spence."

"Well, the man was Spence," Smith intervened. "I saw him jump in the cab myself. I came in here and told you."

He turned to the driver.

"Go on. What happened?"

The chauffeur took a deep breath. "I drive to Calle L. When I stop he says: 'Go in café and get drink and be back in fifteen minutes.' I am thirsty, I say: 'All right.' I go into café and have drink. After fifteen minutes I come back. I get into seat. I start car. Man sitting there. I drive back. I come here." He wiped his forehead. "Ten years I work for Biltmore. Never anything happens to me. Never."

"Go on!" urged Smith.

"I get here," the chauffeur swallowed. "I get out. I open the door. The man do not move. I say something. He say nothing. Then I look. It is terrible! Ten years I work for Biltmore and never anything happen."

But Smith was already out of the door. Breese and I followed him hurriedly.

Seated in the back of the open cab, his hands folded upon his stomach, his long elbows grotesquely akimbo, was a sallow-faced individual, apparently asleep.

"Good God!" cried Breese. "That's Spence—the chap I saw."

Smith looked at him. "Your chauffeur says he told him you sent him away in this cab."

"But I did nothing of the kind," cried Breese. "Why, he left by the back door. He said he'd be gone only a few minutes. I was waiting for him!"

Suddenly the body swayed and then toppled headlong to the floor. The fixed eyes looked directly at us. Then we saw there was a pool of blood upon the seat of the cab.

Breese cried out in horror.

CHAPTER XXIII
CALLE L

ACROWD OF CURIOSITY SEEKERS had gathered about us. Smith tried to shoo them away, but the Havanese are persistent. It is not every day that one is privileged to witness a corpse in a cab. It was with some relief that we hailed the approach of a native policeman.

Smith issued crisp commands to this man. He wanted the body taken to the morgue for the necessary autopsy. It was not to be moved before the medical examiner appeared. Spence's shop was to be sealed and guarded.

The policeman got into the cab and drove it off alone. At this Breese's man set up a wail. He would not part with his beloved car. For ten years he had worked for the Biltmore. His reputation and his cab were both spotless.

But the detective silenced him with a glare and not too ceremoniously hoisted him into another taxi. Smith and I followed.

"You're going to take us to the place where you say you left Spence," Smith informed the driver, who looked mournfully back for his vanished cab. "Savvy?" The driver nodded miserably.

As we approached Calle L, he urged his colleague to slow down. The houses we passed were vaguely familiar, impressive stone houses befitting the aristocratic Vedado quarter. Then he called: "Here! Here!" Our cab stopped.

We had pulled up directly in front of the Gilded Cage!

"Here!" exclaimed the chauffeur, "here this man told me to stop. He looked around for a minute, then he says: 'Go to café.' I go to café on corner. There." He pointed to the modest bodega not far away. "I go inside. I come back." He wrung his hands as he relived the tragedy. "It is terrible. Ten years I work for Biltmore and never anything happen. Never!"

But Smith had gotten out and was studying the Gilded Cage. Breese still sat in the cab, as if in stupefied wonder. But he was roused by Smith's first sharp question.

"You say, Mr. Breese, that you did *not* send this man here?" Smith demanded.

"I certainly did not," declared Breese emphatically.

"Despite what your driver says?"

"Despite what anybody says."

"And yet," Smith said slowly, "he drives to your house."

Smith turned to the driver. "You say you sat in that café for fifteen minutes. Could you see your cab from there?"

"Sure—sure," the driver nodded vigorously. "I watch my cab. I do not leave it alone. I don't know this man."

"You watched that cab all the time?"

"Sure—sure. All the time."

"Now listen to me carefully," Smith urged. "Did you see another man approach your man in the cab?"

"No. No one came to cab. No one."

"There must have been some one," Smith exclaimed impatiently. "The man didn't kill himself."

"No one! No one came to cab," insisted the driver. "I watched. I see. I wonder why he send me away because he just sit there fifteen minutes."

Smith swore softly in his perplexity. "But someone must have shot him," he insisted. "He must have come here to keep a date. He must have been expecting someone. Why did he dismiss you?"

"No one came here," the driver repeated. "I watch."

"We'll see if you did," snapped Smith. "You take us to the chair you occupied in the café. Come on!"

The driver dutifully led us to the bodega and to the seat he had occupied. We got a clear view of both the cab and the street through the broad windows. Further, not only the driver but the swarthy jowelled proprietor and some of his habitual patrons were ready to swear that no one had approached the cab. They had been idly observing it, they said. They remembered it well.

And no one had heard a shot of any kind.

The further we plunged into the circumstances of the third murder associated with the Gilded Cage, the more uncanny it seemed. I know that for my part, although it was broad daylight, a bright sun, a profusion of tropical flowers everywhere about us, I shivered as if I were listening to a ghost story upon a moonless night in some creaky old house.

Smith peered up at the Gilded Cage, as if trying to discover something in its marble walls.

"I've never had a case before," Smith turned to Breese, "that tossed me around the way this one does. I know it all fits together. But I can't tell you how." He paused, observing Breese keenly. "Ordinarily I wouldn't be stumped. I'd hold on to you."

"To me?"

"Yes—if I hold on to you I can puzzle it out."

"But I was with you all the time."

"Yes," said Smith, "but you may have an accomplice. Your driver, for example. Let me show you, Mr. Breese, how guilty you look. Spence is a blackmailer, and you receive a letter from him. Now why does he write you a letter?"

"I don't know," said Breese. "Over the 'phone he said he had information on my wife's death. To my face he said practically nothing, just told me to wait."

"That's your story," said Smith, "but who'd believe it? He wrote me a letter, too. That's natural enough. If his victim didn't come through with money he'd see the police got the information. Now who was his victim? You were the only one, aside from myself, who came to his place. Obviously, he must have had something on you. That's a reasonable conclusion. Particularly in view of the circumstantial evidence against you in the other two cases. Then, your driver says he told him you sent him off in the cab. Where does he go? To your house. And in front of your house he is killed."

"Good God," exclaimed Breese, "you almost convince me it's so!"

"I almost convince myself it's so," said Smith.

"But I assure you——" protested Breese.

"And yet," interrupted Smith, "that doesn't explain how he was murdered by someone unseen and unheard."

"It may have been a silencer," I suggested.

"Undoubtedly," said Smith. "But nobody's invented an invisible gun or an invisible man. Unless——" he stopped suddenly and looked up at the huge shrouded windows of the Gilded Cage. "Unless the executioner," he continued grimly, "was waiting in one of those windows with a gun and silencer." He shouted suddenly. "That's it."

He pointed to one of the windows.

"No doubt of it," he continued excitedly. "A man standing there, at that window—Spence down here in the cab and——"

To our amazement the window swung open. Then we saw a huge head. Perutkin appeared at the window. He was beckoning to Smith, suggesting by signs that he go into the house.

"There's that lunatic again," muttered Breese.

"What's he doing here?" Smith demanded of me. "I'll have to lock him up just to get rid of him."

But the Russian was gesticulating wildly.

"He wants us to come in," I suggested.

"I want to go in anyway," said Smith, moving up the long stairs to the terrace. "He's probably got another hare-brained scheme." He dismissed the Russian from his mind contemptuously. "But that's the explanation. No doubt of it. Spence was killed from a window in this house. Now we'll find out who's in that house and this time I let nobody go."

"But who can it be?" muttered Breese. "Someone I know? Someone in the house, someone with us on the yacht? The mere thought of it is appalling."

We had reached the terrace. The door swung open. The Russian greeted us.

"A thousand pardons, Mr. Smith," he called. "I left you unceremoniously. I plead haste. And a thousand pardons to you, Mr. Breese. I am responsible for any unpleasantness that may have been caused you. I was led astray. I insisted you were a criminal. And I had no evidence. I can only beg your pardon."

"What is it you want now?" Smith insisted grimly. "You've got nothing more to do with this case. You know that, don't you?"

"That is true," replied the Russian, "in half an hour I shall have nothing more to do with this case. Yours shall be the glory, Mr. Smith. The case is over." He paused. "It is too bad about Spence. A blackmailer, but still a human being."

"How do you know about him?" Smith demanded.

"I foresaw his end, poor chap," the Russian sighed. "When I left you so hurriedly I had hoped to prevent it. But when I came here I knew I was too late."

Smith looked at him, shaking his head in baffled wonder.

"You see, it was inevitable," the Russian explained. "Spence was the last. There shall be no more murders. Now there shall be retribution. When Mrs. Breese was killed, it was written that Trenholm should go. And when Trenholm confided in Spence, and Spence very foolishly sought profit from his highly dangerous information, Spence was doomed." He added casually: "But I have our man."

"Which one is it this time?" Smith sneered.

"The right one," replied the Russian. "You need have no fear. I made one mistake in this case, I concede it. I overlooked one slight detail. It entirely escaped me. And that one slight detail sent me off on the wrong track. I became confused. My work was execrable. I can only apologize. But I have made up for it. I have corrected my error. And I have the man you want."

"Is this another one of your experiments?" demanded Smith.

"No," said the Russian. "I have disappointed you before, Mr. Smith. I have disappointed myself. Even now I kick myself violently for my stupidity."

"Well," said Smith practically, "who is it and where is he?"

"Will you give me half an hour—thirty minutes?" asked the Russian.

"I knew there was a catch in it," sighed Smith.

"I could turn the man over to you at this moment," the Russian said, "but it would not be advisable."

Smith shook his head. "I've wasted enough time with you," he said. "If you have anything, come out with it."

"Very well," said the Russian. "You refuse me? Then find the man yourself. I have no self-interest. I am merely helping you. Is a half-hour so precious to you that you cannot gamble it against a certainty? I assume you want the man. I shall get him for you, in exactly thirty minutes. He is not far from you now."

Smith is by nature a trader. He overlooks no bargains. After a moment's hesitation, he said finally: "All right! I'll give you half an hour. If you don't produce, better keep out of my way!"

"Excellent!" exclaimed the Russian. "Come with me!"

CHAPTER XXIV
MODUS OPERANDI

WHEN WE ENTERED THE drawing-room of the Gilded Cage, we found assembled there all our fellow-passengers of the yacht. At first sight, they might have been guests at some informal reception. The Count and Countess were seated close together, chatting amiably enough as we approached. I judged from their expressions that despite the tragedy hovering over them, or because of it, the Count had gone far in his effort at reconciliation in the last few days.

Rice and the younger Breese were standing near the window, conversing in low tones. The actor, as usual, sulked in a corner by himself, smoking a cigarette with the aid of an extraordinarily long amber holder.

Smith had warned Breese outside to mention nothing of the fate that had overtaken Spence. The old man was obviously restrained in greeting his children and Rice. To Thomas he paid no attention whatsoever.

I wondered how the Russian had assembled them all, and for what purpose. I noticed, too, that although the sun was bright outside, the curtains were securely drawn, and the chandelier glowing with light. The room would have been dark without it.

From the Russian's first words, it was obvious that they were waiting for him to proceed with whatever it was he had in mind. He said: "Now we are complete. Mr. Breese is here. Mr. Smith is here." He turned to the detective, took his arm, and led him to the library. I followed curiously. Standing at the door were the Japanese footman and the English butler. Seated at the table was a bespectacled young American, whom the Russian presented as "Mr. Jenkins of the Ministry." We shook hands with this stranger, and I wondered what it all meant.

But the Russian was reserving his explanation for those in the drawing-room. Standing in the center of the room, he rapped twice with his knuckles upon the table for silence.

"Please pay attention!" he called, as if to a group of school children. "You undoubtedly wonder why I summoned you here in the name of the law. I shall tell you. You have come to assist in the administration of justice. I shall ask you all to cooperate with me to the very best of your ability. There are vital issues at stake." He cleared his throat. "What I am about to ask you to do may be distasteful. It may cause some of you real pain. But I wish you to believe that whatever sacrifice you make will not be in vain. Listen to me, please——

"It is the belief of the police that one and the same person killed the late Mrs. Breese, killed the unfortunate wireless operator, Trenholm, and only this afternoon killed the wretched Charles Spence. Some of you may not know it, but a third, and the last of the murders, was committed less than an hour ago in front of this house!"

I heard a buzz of startled conversation. Once more the Russian rapped upon the table.

"Listen to me, please. We are not repeating the unfortunate incident of the yacht. This time we have made more extensive preparations. This time we do not seek the murderer. We know him. Now here is what I wish you to do: Listen carefully: In a few moments, in this room, we are going to reconstruct the murder of Mrs. Breese." He looked at the Countess. "I beg a thousand pardons from the members of her family. I assure them if I could spare them this ordeal, I would. But it is impossible." He swung around to the rest. "It is now nine o'clock at night, a week ago. I have purposely darkened the room, and put on artificial light, to give verity to our scene. I shall ask all of you to repeat your movements of that night—but exactly!"

With the air of an imperious director, he pointed to the Count.

"You, my friend, at nine o'clock, were where?"

"Outside in the corridor," replied the Count.

"Go there," the Russian commanded. "And do exactly what you did that night. Observe what you observed that night and report to us from the corridor what you see."

Without waiting for the Count to leave, the Russian turned to the Countess and the younger Breese. "You two were upstairs in your rooms. Will you please go there now and come down when the butler calls you, as he called you that night?"

"Look here," the boy protested, "what's the sense of it?"

"I assure you," said the Russian, "I would not dream of subjecting you to this ordeal if it were not extremely necessary."

The boy shrugged his shoulders and followed his sister out of the room.

"It is good they are not here to watch everything," the Russian commented as they left. "I wish to spare them pain." He turned to the father. "You, Mr. Breese, go out into the street, and enter as you did last night. You have your key?"

"Yes," said Breese. "But why the devil should I?"

"Because you wish to clear your name," said the Russian. "I beg of you to do this for your own sake. I have only half an hour. It goes very quickly. Come!"

Reluctantly Breese left the room.

"Now," said the Russian, "I shall take the part of Mrs. Breese. You, Mr. Thomas, were in this room with her. You remain here."

He looked at the actor quizzically.

"You should find this work easy. It is your profession."

Then he raised his voice to its terrific boom: "All of you, everywhere. It is nine o'clock. We begin!"

Then he stared at Rice. "I had quite forgotten you, Mr. Rice. You were at the American Minister's at the time. Very well then. We shall call the library the Ministry. You shall wait there."

Rice good-naturedly nodded, and passed into the library.

"Now," said the Russian to Thomas. "I am Mrs. Breese. We are talking together. What is it you say to me?"

"Hang it all," cried the actor. "I can't remember."

"Say something—anything," commanded the Russian sharply. "Tell me you're going back to the States to marry another girl. I get quite angry. I storm at you, don't I?"

"Yes," the actor swallowed.

"That is better," commented the Russian, stepping out of his rôle. "You actually quarrelled with Mrs. Breese."

"But—but—" stammered the actor.

The Russian held up his hand. "Play your part!" he commanded. "You are an execrable actor. I say to you: 'You have deceived me. I love you.' And you say to me——"

The actor shifted uncomfortably.

"What is it you say to me?"

"Hang it all," he began.

"You say nothing. You storm out of the room. You run upstairs. Go!"

Thomas fled from the room. It was really very funny, but none of us laughed. The Russian had us in his grip.

"You see," said the Russian, "this is what actually happened. Thomas told us fairy tales."

He snorted.

"As if Mrs. Breese would calmly consent to his jilting her."

He turned to the door.

"Count!" he cried. "You are in the corridor. What do you see?"

"I see Mr. Breese coming toward the drawing-room."

"Good," approved the Russian. "Where is the Japanese? Here, you——"

The footman appeared from the library. Evidently the Russian had already given him minute instructions. He entered and picked up a tray from the table.

"Mrs. Breese want nothing more?"

"No," replied the Russian. The footman bowed and obediently returned to the library with his tray.

"Now I am left alone," the Russian said to Smith. "I walk about. I am quite upset by the words of Mr. Thomas. I do not know what to do. My vanity is hurt. The telephone rings. Mr. Rice!"

The promoter appeared from the library. He watched the Russian tolerantly.

"Mr. Rice," commanded the Russian briskly, "you are at the ministry. You are talking over the telephone with Mrs. Breese. Stand where you are, and I shall stand here. I say 'Hello.'"

"Well, it's sort of hard to repeat the exact words," Rice complained. "But I'll do my best. Something like this: 'Hello, Dora, how are you?'"

"Excellent, Mr. Rice. You are our best actor. 'Hello, Gordon.'"

"'Dora, I've some bad news for you.'

"'What is it?'

"'Are you alone?'

"'Yes.'

"'I've just gotten a check from the bank. It's made out to Thomas and your signature is forged to it.'

"'I can't believe it.'

"As a matter of fact," Rice interrupted, "she said much more than that. She railed at me considerably for libelling Mr. Thomas. Finally I said: 'Well, you can see for yourself. I left the check and the letter from the bank teller on the table in the drawing-room!'

"'Very well. Hold the wire. I'll see.'

"Then I waited," said Rice.

"'I can't find it,'" the Russian suggested.

"'That's funny. I put the check and a letter on the table, addressed to you. Thomas must have found it.'

"'I don't believe a word of it!'"

"What's that?" said Rice, looking up startled.

"I was playing my part," the Russian smiled. "Then, I presume, Mrs. Breese hung up suddenly, as startled people will. Good!" He swung around to us. "Now I am left alone once more. I am further distressed. I don't know what to do. Mr. Breese! Where are you?"

"Right outside the door," the financier replied.

"Come in."

The Russian suddenly fell to the floor. The door opened. Breese looked down and started.

"Come closer," the Russian called without shifting. "This is how you found me."

"Yes," said Breese huskily.

"And then you ran out."

"Yes."

"Follow out your movements then, Mr. Breese. Go into the street. Just as you did that night."

Breese hurried out of the room.

"Brandlock," the Russian called to the butler, who hurried forward now. He looked slightly askance at the prone figure of Perutkin. "Come—come—don't be a fool!" the Russian snapped at him. "You saw Mrs. Breese in this position. Run upstairs now as you did then and summon the children."

The butler shrugged his shoulders disdainfully but did as he was told.

The Russian called out into the corridor: "Count, what do you see?"

"I see Mr. Breese running out into the street. I hear the butler telling them upstairs that Mrs. Breese was murdered."

"Good!" exclaimed the Russian. "Which tells us why our friend, the Count, made his foolish confession." He picked himself up from the floor, just as the Breese children ran in.

"Come in, all of you!" he cried. "We need go no further with this. The children run down. They summon a policeman. Someone telephones Rice at the Ministry. So far, we have traced the movements of each known individual. Mr. Thomas leaves in a huff. The telephone rings. Mrs. Breese answers. Mr. Breese comes in and finds his wife dead. The essential moment that still remains to be explained away is the time between Rice's call and the entrance of Mr. Breese. What happened in that moment? What did Mrs. Breese do? How did she meet her death? Look around this room and tell me, Mr. Smith."

"I don't know," said Smith curtly. "And I don't see that this is getting us anywhere."

"You do not see it?" persisted the Russian. "Miraculous! But then, for a long time I did not see it myself." He turned abruptly. "The reason I am reconstructing this crime is to check back upon the known facts. For example, we know now that Mr. Thomas had been quarrelling with Mrs. Breese. We know now that Mr. Breese discovered the body. Now, Mr. Rice?"

"Yes, sir," said the promoter. "Anything further I can do?"

"I want you to refresh your memory and tell us if there's anything you have omitted in your telephone conversation with Mrs. Breese."

The promoter reflected a moment and then shook his head vigorously. "No, I guess not. I guess I covered the ground pretty thoroughly."

"You have forgotten nothing?"

"Not a thing," said Rice emphatically.

"Very well," said the Russian quietly, moving to the library. "Come here, Mr. Jenkins."

CHAPTER XXV
THE CALL

THE BESPECTACLED YOUNG MAN approached Perutkin rather timidly.

"Do you know Mr. Jenkins, Mr. Rice?"

"Afraid I don't," said the promoter. "I just noticed him in the library."

"Mr. Jenkins," said the Russian, "is employed at the American Ministry."

He swung at Rice sharply.

"Are you sure you have omitted nothing in your conversation?"

"Positive," said Rice. "Of course, I may have said something trivial—unessential——"

"Every detail is important," insisted the Russian. "I have done an amount of inquiry in this case, which is stupendous. Most of the information I have gathered is valueless. For example, I wanted to know exactly what it was you said to Mrs. Breese over the telephone that night, and for that reason I questioned Mr. Jenkins."

He turned to the timid young man. "You were at the American Ministry when Mr. Rice telephoned, were you not?"

"Yes, sir, I was."

"And you overheard the conversation?"

"I overheard Mr. Rice's end of it," the young man corrected precisely.

"And does it check with his version today?"

"No, sir."

"What's that?" cried Rice.

"Please be quiet, Mr. Rice," admonished Perutkin. "This is a mere formality. It may have been an oversight on your part. Mr. Jenkins, tell us what Mr. Rice said to Mrs. Breese."

"Well, as I explained to you," began the young man, "I was in the next booth, trying to call my mother. We have two booths at the Ministry. I was waiting for my number. I heard Mr. Rice talking—I couldn't help hearing—and I thought the conversation so peculiar that I remembered it."

The young man stammered in his earnestness.

"I didn't hear anything about—about a check. I heard Mr. Rice say: 'Hello, Dora. How are you?' And then: 'That lecture on companionate marriage. It's starting now. Are you alone?' And then she said something. And he said: 'You'll find it interesting.' Then he said: 'Sixty.' Just the number—'sixty'."

"So!" said the Russian. "A lecture on companionate marriage. Starting now. Sixty."

"Yes, sir."

Rice stared at the clerk.

"I did forget that!" he exclaimed. "I suppose it was so trivial it just slipped my mind. Mrs. Breese was interested in companionate marriage and the Minister happened to mention that some silly woman or other was lecturing on it for the Woman's Club, which, if I remember, is at Malecon 60. I must have repeated this information to Mrs. Breese."

"So!" said the Russian. "It is always advisable to check up on every little detail, no matter how trivial. Mrs. Breese asked you where on the Malecon was the Woman's Club. And you said 'Sixty'."

"Exactly," confirmed Rice.

"When did you say you telephoned Mrs. Breese? At about nine-thirty?"

"Yes. Around nine-thirty."

"Lectures usually start at eight-thirty. It would take her at least half an hour to get to the Malecon from her home, assuming that she started right out, which a woman would not be likely to do. Didn't it occur to you that the lecture would be over by the time she got there?"

Rice shook his head. "Frankly, I didn't think of it. I didn't give the matter sufficient attention. I just thought I'd pass the information on."

"So that the strange conversation that Mr. Jenkins overheard was nothing more than a piece of stray news that you were relaying to Mrs. Breese for no purpose whatsoever?"

"If you want to take it that way," said Rice. "Yes. Honestly, I don't see what you're driving at."

I could see from Smith's expression that the detective agreed with him. But Perutkin was inexorable.

"Let us continue," he said sharply. "I want to ask you a question."

"By all means," Rice invited, smiling tolerantly.

"Are you a wealthy man, Mr. Rice?"

"Well," Rice hesitated. "I wouldn't say that."

The Russian swung at the elder Breese.

"You, Mr. Breese, know the extent of Mr. Rice's finances. He has always been more or less in your employ. Would you call him a wealthy man?"

"I'm afraid I'll have to leave that to Mr. Rice," Breese replied. "I don't see what his wealth has to do with the murder of my wife."

"Only this," said the Russian, "I was always under the impression that Mr. Rice was independently wealthy. Therefore, I could not understand his movements. Now I can."

He paused, while we all looked at Rice in bewilderment. He flushed uncomfortably.

"I don't see how my finances concern you," he said with some asperity.

"Enough!" cried the Russian suddenly. "I shall ask no more questions. Why should I? I do not seek information. I know. Mr. Rice, will you go to the radio and turn the dial until you reach the number sixty?"

The Russian moved to the black and silver radio. He tapped it with his great knuckles. "A beautiful instrument. I desire, Mr. Rice, that you tune in on sixty."

"What for?" said Rice.

"We are reconstructing the murder of Mrs. Breese," replied the Russian. "This radio is in exactly the condition and position that it was on that night. I have seen to that. Will you turn the dial to sixty, Mr. Rice?"

Rice made no move.

"I am giving you your opportunity," the Russian said softly. "I am being merciful. Turn that dial to sixty."

Rice, as if hypnotized, shuffled towards the radio. His entire demeanor had changed. His shoulders drooped, his face was ashen. Rarely have I seen such a picture of defeat.

Now his hand was upon the dial.

"Sixty," repeated the Russian.

The hand moved, slowly. Suddenly a flash of fire came from the radio. Rice fell to the floor.

I could not but gasp in horror. Then, shuddering, I saw the Russian deliberately kick the prone body. The Russian was shaking with laughter.

"Get up!" he thundered. "Do you think I'd give you up so easily? I put blanks in, Mr. Rice. *You did not!*"

CHAPTER XXVI
THE RUSSIAN EXPLAINS

THE RUSSIAN BEAMED UPON the dazed and frightened circle about him.

"I have given you," he said with his characteristic pedantic air, "a concrete demonstration of the *modus operandi* of as ingenious and carefully planned a crime as it has been my privilege to study. I realize that to some of you the subject has been extremely painful."

He looked at Mary Breese paternally.

"But even you, Miss Breese, and your family should find consolation in the thought that the man responsible for the tragedy in your lives has finally been brought to punishment." He turned abruptly to Rice. "Will you care to explain the reasons for your horrible crimes, or shall I do it?"

Rice looked down at the floor. Outwardly he had recovered his composure. His face was a mask.

"Very well," said the Russian. "I shall be content with second-hand information and guesswork, since you will not oblige. Now, Miss Breese and gentlemen, we must first enter into the motives that prompted the first of Mr. Rice's crimes. It is my guess that Mr. Rice deserted you, Mr. Breese, during the unpleasantness of the divorce trial at his own suggestion. He suggested to you that if he became Mrs. Breese's business adviser, he could keep an eye out for your interests. He might even be able to patch up your domestic differences. Am I right?"

"Yes," said Breese, staring incredulously at Rice while he answered. "He did suggest just that."

"His real reason, of course," continued the Russian, "was to get his hands on Mrs. Breese's extensive properties. Mr. Rice was a promoter by trade and a soldier of fortune by inclination. We must go deeply into his character to understand and appreciate his motives. Until the time he met you in Paris, Mr. Breese, he had led a hand to mouth existence. Association with you helped him float a few ventures, some of them successful, some of them failures. His ambition was boundless."

"You asked him to Riga. It is my theory, Mr. Rice, that you were acquainted with the Baron Peter Setovski before you met him in Riga on the occasion of the marriage of my friend, the Count, to Miss Breese. I cannot prove it. It is my guess that the Baron knew of some disreputable incident—one of many—in your past, and threatened to expose you to Mr. Breese. You took an effective way out, and my friend, the Count, was implicated. This is only a theory. I cannot prove it. Perhaps you care to comment, Mr. Rice?"

But the promoter looked disdainfully at him and said nothing.

"Very well," the Russian shrugged his shoulders. "We leave theory and proceed to facts. For a long time I was led astray in this case by a series of suspicious circumstances that signified nothing. It so happens that any human being is capable of murder under certain circumstances. Otherwise, no murder would remain unsolved. All murderers would be labelled, or even licensed. But I joke. It is in bad taste.

"In this case, we were faced with the problem of a very unusual woman. She had been separated from her husband, and attached herself to a worthless young man who has not been even faithful to her. It was only natural that suspicion should seek out these two. Mr. Smith chose one suspect. And I the other.

"I say nothing of my friend, the Count. He managed to confuse us for but an instant with his confession. He, too, suspected the elder Breese and sought to protect the father of the girl he loves.

"Now I am frank to say that until the murder of the wireless operator, I was completely lost in this case. Inexcusably so. But then my brain recovered its strength. I ploughed ahead. After all, it was obvious. Behold! Of all those who knew and might have killed Mrs. Breese, only one was absent from the house at the time. He was equipped with a magnificent alibi. He was dining at the American Minister's.

"I thought to myself: 'Suppose I wanted to murder this woman! What would be my first move?' Naturally, my first move would be to protect myself. Mr. Thomas made no such move. Mr. Breese made no such move. Then I thought to myself: 'What is the best way of protecting oneself while committing murder?' And my logical brain replied: 'By not being present at the scene of the crime.'

"But you would say that is impossible. No. Then one must seek an accomplice. I worked on that basis for many days, looking for the accomplice. Naturally, when Trenholm was killed, I judged immediately that he was the accomplice. But no one saw Trenholm near the scene of the crime. I could not understand it.

"Then I delved into Trenholm's background. He was a wireless operator. He was a mechanic. I sought any and every possible means of connecting him with this house. Methodically by elimination, I finally came to the radio set. I saw light.

"Remember, Trenholm never met Mrs. Breese. He was but recently engaged for the yacht. At this point, I must interrupt myself to say that the mechanical murder is not unfamiliar to me. It is the refuge of either cowards or master criminals. In my country, bombs have been placed in pianos, and even attached to typewriters. But these devices make fearful noise, and are open to detection.

"So it remained for our friend, Rice, to single out Mr. Trenholm. What his arguments were I do not know, and it does not matter. In any case, this is what Mr. Trenholm did for Mr. Rice." The Russian pulled open the case of the radio. "Mr. Trenholm took an ordinary revolver, equipped with a silencer, quite common these days. He placed it upon this small stand. He built a lever, a small piece of metal, connecting with the dial and the trigger of the revolver. Come closer and you shall see. The revolver is no longer loaded. Observe that when the dial comes to sixty, the lever has pressed the trigger back and the revolver explodes. Observe that the weapon is so placed in the aperture for the loud speaker that its explosion leaves no mark upon the instrument.

"Simple, is it not? Now, Mr. Rice had, as I have indicated, certain reasons for ridding himself of Mrs. Breese. He had been her business adviser, and consequently handled her funds. Unfortunately, Mr. Rice diverted these funds to his own use, and some of his ventures and speculations were unsuccessful.

"At this very time, Mrs. Breese proposed to marry the actor, Thomas. Naturally, Mr. Rice is opposed to any man entering the establishment. It will weaken his power. But not only does Mrs. Breese plan a second marriage, but, with her characteristic dominance, proposes to manage her own affairs. Mr. Rice is in a dilemma. He cannot tell Mrs. Breese that he has tied up all her money in his own ventures. Mrs. Breese becomes obstinate.

"An ordinary man would have broken down and confessed. But Rice has the soul of the born adventurer and gambler. Pressed to the wall, he thinks how convenient it would be if Mrs. Breese were out of the way. He knows that she has left a will naming him as executor. He wants none of her money. He has it. All he seeks is to retain his unquestioned control.

"So he plans. First, he angles for an invitation to dinner at the American Minister's. No alibi could be more substantial or impressive. Then he arranges the radio, and takes care to let everyone except Mrs. Breese know that it needs repair, and should not be tampered with. Then he arranges to telephone Mrs. Breese and, ascertaining that she is alone, tells her to tune in on her favorite hobby, companionate marriage. He hangs up. He is safe. Mrs. Breese goes to the radio, turns to sixty as she was instructed and is killed.

"Mr. Rice rightly figures that the police will not examine the contents of the radio set. It is an easy matter for him to remove the weapon at the first opportunity.

"But all crimes have their complications. Whatever it was that Mr. Rice told Trenholm when he first ordered his diabolical mechanical murderer, there seems to be no question that Trenholm guessed or knew that he was indirectly responsible for the death of Mrs. Breese.

"Trenholm is timid. Like most mechanics, he has a hard-grained uprightness in his soul. His conscience troubles him. Although Trenholm made few acquaintances, he did strike up a friendship with one of his own kind, the mechanic Spence, who ran a bicycle shop. In a burst of confidence, Trenholm tells Spence exactly what has occurred. But Spence has no false ideas of morals. He sees it as a golden opportunity to milk Rice.

"Behold! We come to the night of the funeral on the yacht. Hitherto, Trenholm has been free from all police surveillance. On that night he is plunged into the melodramatic third-degree to which we subjected all of you. Rice is shrewd enough to see that it is all a plan, a trick. But Trenholm is nervous. Rice determines to get rid of Trenholm. He must, otherwise Trenholm will expose him. So Rice picks Mr. Smith's pocket, shoots Trenholm and then puts the revolver back in my colleague's pocket.

"Then Rice feels free. At last his crime is covered. He can leave the country. All will be well. Incidentally, some of his ventures have now recovered. He will be able to straighten out the estate. There is not a breath of suspicion.

"Out of clear sky comes a telephone call from Spence, and instantly Rice realizes that Trenholm has been talking. His work is not yet over. Rice is in a frenzy. Spence wants enormous sums of money. Rice is adventurer enough to know you cannot ever pay a blackmailer. The process is continuous.

"I do not think Mr. Rice enjoyed his crimes. I do not think he is possessed with any insane relish of homicide. Mr. Rice may be brutal, but he is not a killer by instinct. I am willing to say that the prospect of a third murder made Mr. Rice feel very unpleasant.

"He tried to bluff Spence out, but the young man was too shrewd. He sent a letter to you, Mr. Breese, so that he could telephone Rice that unless he got his money he would expose to you what had happened. Rice, upon receiving this intelligence, instructed him to get into a cab and come to this house. He told him to dismiss his driver, and that he would then receive the money.

"Of course, Rice went to a window with the revolver he had taken from the radio. He used a silencer, so no one could hear. He fired one bullet. It struck Mr. Spence and silenced him forever. Then Mr. Rice was done."

He looked at the promoter reflectively. "You had only intended one perfect crime. But it resolved itself into three. The second, of Trenholm, was not half bad. The third was atrocious. You should have realized that suspicion would point to someone in this house. You should have realized that I was at work. However, it is always the way with criminals. They are brilliant only in flashes. Eventually they must lower the quality of their work, and they are caught."

"I don't suppose," said Rice grimly, "there's any need of my saying anything."

"Quite the contrary," replied the Russian. "You may contribute something vitally interesting. My recital was necessarily bald, and in spots guesswork. Only the essentials are indisputable. Your confession would be extremely interesting to Mr. Smith and myself."

"Sure," agreed Smith. "Only there's no need of making it here. We'll take you down to Headquarters if you don't mind, Mr. Rice."

"Very well," said Rice, extending his hands. Smith produced a pair of shining handcuffs.

Then I saw Rice jump suddenly, and with both hands push Smith violently to the floor. The next moment the promoter had leaped through the closed window, with a wild smash of glass.

The Russian jumped after him. Smith picked himself up from the floor. In one hand he held a revolver. He followed the Russian out of the window.

Then we heard two shots in rapid succession. Then two more.

I ran out into the garden. The street was buzzing with people. I turned to find the Russian beside me.

"It does not matter," he said. "I leave to Mr. Smith the punishment. I am interested only in the solution. Do I not deserve to be congratulated? Have I not done an extraordinary piece of detective work? Am I not the greatest detective in the world?"

He looked down into the street.

"Ah! I see Mr. Rice. Mr. Smith has apparently aimed well. Mr. Rice has not escaped. Well, it is all one to me. Mr. Smith will undoubtedly write himself an impressive report. He will miss the glory of the trial. But what of me? What am I to do? What shall occupy this brain of mine? It is a sad world, my friend, when a detective cannot find work. I am very sad. And when I am sad, I drink champagne. Nothing but champagne. Come!"

www.ingramcontent.com/pod-product-compliance
Lightning Source LLC
Chambersburg PA
CBHW011447170626
46816CB00008B/2566